RACING FOR LOVE

JAYNE RYLON

RACING FOR LOVE

Published by Happy Endings Publishing

Edited by Mary Moran

Cover Art by Angela Waters

Formatted by IRONHORSE Formatting

Driven

Shifting Gears

www.jaynerylon.com

Facebook.com/jaynerylon

@JayneRylon on Twitter

ISBN-13: 978-1-941785-04-1

Contents

DRIVEN

JAYNE RYLON

Dedication

I'd like to give a shout out the girls I met in the bathroom of the Harrisburg, PA airport when our flight was diverted from NYC. Thanks for offering to split a limo with me so we could all get to Broadway on time. The front row seats were worth it!

CHAPTER ONE

"Ladies and gentleman, this is your captain speaking."

Lynn Madison strained to hear the distorted announcement despite the shitty airplane speakers and the baby who'd been screaming since they'd taken off over an hour ago. She didn't blame the munchkin. She would bawl too if she didn't get that the gray clouds causing the turbulence, which bounced their regional jet across the sky, weren't as ominous as they appeared.

"We've been in a holding pattern, circling New York for the past fifteen minutes. Air traffic control just radioed. They're closing the airport until this cell blows over. No one's allowed in or out. We'll be diverting to Harrisburg, Pennsylvania but the delay shouldn't cost us more than an hour."

Groans of disappointment and frustration drowned out the sporadic whispers of concern proliferated by less-seasoned fliers. Lynn jumped straight to rearranging her tight schedule in her mind as the pilot droned on.

"We'll grab some fuel then wait for an update. If the situation changes, we'll let you know. We should be on the ground in about twenty minutes. Thank you for your patience. Be sure to keep your seat belt fastened; the air will be bumpy during our descent. Flight attendants, please prepare for landing."

Before the beady-eyed flight attendant could scold Lynn about stowing her netbook, she clicked to her browser window then hopped on the *Tempt the Cougar* blog she shared with a circle of friends. Her college roommate Rachel had introduced her to the group of erotic romance enthusiasts after Lynn had bitched about her bland sex life. The ladies had recommended several novels that had her eyebrows climbing and her fantasies growing spicier by the minute.

They'd quickly become very close, welcoming her into the fold and encouraging her to follow their lead in prowling for a younger man to seduce. She had to admit, the stories she'd heard since hanging around them had inspired some wicked fantasies.

Lynn envied the women who'd found love along with their wild adventures. But their proactive attitude in snatching the reins of their lives had resonated with her more than their steamy affairs. Enough to spur her to some serious introspection on what she wanted to do with the rest of her time on earth.

She'd set up a get-together with the members who lived in the tristate region while she killed time during her layover. She hadn't wanted to wait until next year's RomantiCon to meet them in person.

Thank God she'd splurged on the in-flight Wi-Fi.

LynnLuvs2Travel: Only have a few seconds, ladies. Flight is being diverted due to weather. Looks like I might have to bail on dinner. Was so looking forward to it! Sorry ☹ Expecting an update when we land. Fingers crossed I don't miss my connection to Europe!!!

Lynn sighed as she snapped the lid closed then tucked the netbook into her seatback pocket. Figured this would happen on the first day of her new life. The monumental changes she'd implemented had almost seemed too easy so far. Like blowing out the single candle that had topped the cake Rachel had baked for Lynn's fortieth birthday.

In the instant before she'd snuffed the flame, she'd wished her destiny were her own. No more wasted years, working on someone else's clock. Figuring out what she'd rather do, since retiring early would mean living in a cardboard box for twenty years or so until her investments kicked in, had taken a bit longer. But not much.

Three months later, she'd quit her job as a sourcing agent for a high-end retailer. Instant lightness had pervaded her soul when she turned in her resignation, reaffirming her decision.

After a dozen years of dreadful stays in spartan hotels, eating meat-and-potato meals or hauling ass through sketchy parts of foreign cities—all on the recommendation of her male counterparts—she knew better than most that a series of travel guides aimed at professional women going solo constituted an undiscovered niche in the market. It wasn't that the guys had deliberately sabotaged her, but her priorities ran more to a clean room, a spa and healthy meals than the number of strip clubs in a half-mile radius or a smoky bar with nonstop sports playing on a bazillion flat screen TVs.

Preoccupied with reliving the whirlwind of the past couple weeks, she was surprised at the squeak of the wheels meeting the runway.

As soon as she peered through the fogged plastic porthole to the tarmac, she abandoned hope. No fewer than a dozen jets kept their stranded plane company. Even if the sun shone bright at JFK in the next half-hour, the snafu had induced a logistics nightmare.

Sure enough, the pilot emerged from the cockpit to address the cabin face-to-face. "I'm sorry, folks, but things look worse than we originally thought. Traffic is being rerouted along the entire East Coast. We're going to let you head into the terminal until we receive a better estimate on our revised departure time."

Lynn's heart raced in her chest. She had lived well within her means despite her hefty corporate paycheck. The nest egg she'd accumulated had supplied her a shot at pursuing her dream but, in this economy, she'd had a hell of a time securing outside investors to back a no-name upstart. If the delay caused her and several hundred other people to camp out and compete for the limited vacant spots on cramped international flights, her itinerary could be ruined.

Everything hinged on making it to her starting point as scheduled. Train passes, local guides, connections, sold-out hotels…

The idea of all the lost work, not to mention cash for the original reservations and the last-minute bookings, had tears stinging her eyes. Would her old job consider rehiring her if this venture flopped? Probably not.

She gathered her belongings then filed down the stairs onto the tarmac for the march into the dinky terminal. On top of everything else, they had to be stranded at a two-gate airport with rudimentary facilities and limited options for connections.

Note to self... Include a chapter on travelers' insurance and the appropriate amount of time to leave between flights. Not that the six hours she'd allotted would help much in this situation. The insurance policy she'd selected would cover her flight arrangements if necessary but nothing could recoup the lost time. She'd have to drop chapters of her book.

As the herd of disgruntled passengers trundled up the ramp into the steel and glass building, which seemed out of place in the surrounding fields, they merged with the unfortunate occupants of the other impacted flights. A red-faced man doused in cheap cologne yelled into his Blackberry. He cut her off in his dash to hit up the airline representatives waiting inside. He rammed into her shoulder, knocking her oversized purse containing her netbook onto her elbow. The shifting weight threw her off balance on the slick surface.

Lynn skidded several feet toward the railing before a warm, muscled arm wrapped around her waist and a grumpy mumble washed over her earlobe. "Asshole."

She flinched, attempting to shy away. "What is wrong with people? I tripped."

One touch from an unknown man and she just about swallowed her tongue despite his rude treatment. *Lame!*

A carefree laugh replaced the foul temper she'd attempted to deflect. "Sorry, gorgeous. Not you. I meant that asshole who shoved you. He's lucky I don't kick his inconsiderate ass."

Her imagination ran wild at his tone—confident, worldly, bold, gallant but not too stuffy. The midnight voice colored by subtle hints of a Mediterranean accent inspired a million dirty thoughts that had her squirming. The broad hand on her ribs flexed so close to her breast she sucked in a gasp, willing her nipples to stop hardening beneath her thin, silk blouse.

"Damn, are you hurt?" He spun her into the shelter of his arms, his palms bracing her shoulders.

So young! Heat blossomed in her cheeks. Here she was,

lusting after a man at least a decade younger than her who probably thought himself a good Samaritan for helping his elder. As quick as she chastised herself, a naughty whisper invaded her embarrassment. *The Cougar ladies had scored men like this. Those lucky bitches!*

Hell, some of them had even managed to bag *two* virile studs.

"Let me help you inside."

Did he think her deaf and dumb on top of clumsy after that giant space out?

"I'm fine. Really." She shrugged from his hold, instantly regretting the loss of his touch. Her skin tingled where his fingers had rested. "Thank you."

"Any time."

She picked up the pace to avoid an awkward silence as he shuffled along next to her through the crowd, but he somehow managed to dodge a harried mom pushing a double stroller, a gentleman wrestling with a cello and a couple holding hands to keep even with her.

In her peripheral vision, she admired the agile maneuvers of his lean but built body. His black duffle, peppered with logos, rode against a trim hip covered in the dark navy denim favored by recent trends. The lighter creases around his upper thighs led her straight to dangerous territory. She jerked her gaze upward but had to cant her head pretty far to glimpse his unruly brown waves beneath a red baseball cap with something embroidered on the front.

His scruffy jaw couldn't obscure his sculpted cheekbones. The shadowed skin highlighted the contrast of his bright blue eyes. The impact of his stunning looks almost had her tripping again. It'd been fifteen years since she'd gotten her hands on prime beef like that.

Lynn Marie, how crass! Maybe the Cougars really were rubbing off on her.

"So, where were you headed?" No hint of exertion roughened his tone. Funny, her heart beat as hard as if she'd run a marathon.

"JFK."

"Me too." A grimace tugged his stunning mouth into a scowl.

They emerged from the Jetway into a tiny holding area crammed beyond capacity. Instead of wasting time at the airline's inundated desk, she headed for the departure board. Mr. Young-'n'-Sexy followed two steps behind. She adjusted her bag to cover her ass then tugged the hem of her skirt lower on her thighs when she sensed his stare on them. No use in advertising her sag.

Damn it, she couldn't remember the last time she'd fallen victim to an attraction so sudden and fierce. Of course, she had to waste it on someone out of her league whom she'd never see again after these five minutes fate had thrust them together passed.

The red status lights painting the departure and arrival board into a facsimile of something out of Amsterdam's infamous district had her heart plummeting. Every flight originating east of the Mississippi had been cancelled.

For three seconds, she forgot all about the hunk.

"Looks like we're going nowhere fast." The guy shoved his hat from his head, scrubbing his fingers through the thick mass of his luscious hair.

"I have five hours until my connection, maybe it'll clear up by then."

He scrunched his nose and gave his head a tiny shake but stopped short of contradicting her. Probably because he saw her fingernails gouging her palm around the strap of her bag.

"Maybe."

Lynn peered at the churning mass of people—all talking at once, calling loved ones or scrambling to make alternate arrangements—while she searched for a place to sit. Maybe if she could get online she would find some updated info. When two men in business suits abandoned a bench nearby, she plopped onto it. Electric sparks shot along her leg when the hottie perched beside her, their knees touching.

"I'm Sebastian, by the way." He tossed her a dazzling grin as he dug in his pocket for his neon green smartphone. When he leaned to the side for better access, he invaded her personal space in ways that had a riot of butterflies taking flight in her stomach. His chest, covered in snug gray t-shirt with faded charcoal designs, pressed close.

If she turned a teensy bit she could imagine herself in his arms. If she lifted her face an inch or two he would have easy access to claim her lips. Not that he'd want to. A man like him must have women falling all over him. Younger, more beautiful women. Women who'd have some clue of what to do with a sex god. Women who weren't afraid to go after what they wanted.

She cleared her throat then fished out her netbook. "I'm Lynn."

"Pretty. It fits."

Did she imagine the flare of desire in his amazing eyes? She could have stared into them all day if his phone hadn't chosen then to buzz as whoever he'd whipped off a text message to must have responded. Probably his girlfriend *du jour* or a booty call he'd stand up in New York.

The website for her airline had crashed by the time she remembered what she'd been doing. No doubt due to the thousands of people in situations as urgent as hers within a six-state radius. She clicked refresh then sighed as the browser's progress icon spun and spun. No hope for it.

While she waited, she tried to ignore the growling of her stomach drowning out the click of Sebastian typing fast and furious with his thumbs. In anticipation of her rich dinner at the swank Manhattan restaurant, she'd skipped breakfast.

"Will you hold my spot for a minute?" He patted the bench as he rose, leaving his bag behind.

Lynn couldn't resist teasing him. "Well, you don't look like a terrorist but I'm not sure I can vouch for the contents of your unattended bag."

"Gorgeous, you're welcome to peek at my underwear if you like but I won't stay away from the most beautiful woman in Harrisburg more than two minutes. Tops. You can time me." She had no doubt he intended the racy implications of his smoky tone when he paired it with a wink that melted her insides.

Her tongue almost dragged the floor as she watched his tight ass flex in time to his strut until he faded into the crowd.

Screw the airline's site, she needed reinforcements. Fast.

LynnLuvs2Travel: OMG! Still stuck in the airport, no hope for making dinner. Hottest guy ever rescued me from splattering on the runway. Now sitting next to me since he's heading to JFK too. You all are a bad influence! I can't stop thinking about what he'd be like in bed. Blue, blue eyes. Body to die for. Sexy accent. Killer smile. God, he even smells good. I think I might have had a mini orgasm just looking at him. Too bad he's probably not even thirty yet.

She'd barely hit the send button when a flashing box with Rachel's name appeared on her screen like magic.

Rachel: Make lemonade!

LynnLuvs2Trvl: Yeah, I'm thinking of heading to Hertz to rent a car. Pulled up driving directions. I think I can make it if I go right now. Checking the budget first but...that's what credit cards are for, right?

Rachel: LYNN!!!! I meant your stud! This is exactly what you need. Someone to help you shake things up. Match your love life to your new career.

LynnLuvs2Trvl: What? Are you kidding? I have so much riding on this trip. I can't risk it on a guy who's not going to give me the time of day.

Rachel: You know I respect the hard decisions you've made lately, sweetie. But really, you're not going to be happy until you go for broke. It's not only your job that stifled you. It was those boring men you dated. You have to stop settling for safe.

LynnLuvs2Trvl: Maybe, but not now.

Rachel: Then when? I haven't heard you talk about a man like that in...well...ever!

LynnLuvs2Trvl: It's crazy. From the first moment he touched me, my system went haywire.

Rachel: I know exactly what you mean. It's like that for me with Ethan. Please don't throw that away. Please. Go rent your car. But...ask him if he wants a ride! I bet you a triple chocolate sundae he says yes so fast your head will spin.

LynnLuvs2Trvl: Drive four hours with a complete stranger? Have you lost your mind?

Rachel: It's possible. Trust your instincts. You always have been a good judge of character.

LynnLuvs2Trvl: You're corrupting me. I can't believe I actually considered that for two seconds. No way, Rach. Sorry, I have to go. Have to get this mess straightened out before all my plans are ruined.

Rachel: Okay, sweetie. I hope it works out! And if you miss your flight, then I hope he has a twin brother and you let both guys sweep you off your feet to live out your wildest and craziest ménage fantasies. Come to the dark side. Go Team Cougar!

LynnLuvs2Trvl: LOL Love you, crazycakes.

Rachel: Love you too. Let me know how it goes.

Chapter Two

"Either you found out our flights are on track again or your boyfriend sent you one hell of an email." Sebastian cursed the unfamiliar jealousy streaking through him over the naughty grin decorating the sinful lips of the woman he'd just met. "Since I didn't hear any cheering from the rest of these folks, I'm betting on the boyfriend."

Damn though, she'd drawn him to her like the strongest magnet on earth. Something about her sang to him, irresistible and potent. Sure, she was smoking hot. Fine. Her ash blonde hair framed her elegant face in soft curtains and her mile-high heels accentuated her long legs, but that alone couldn't account for the hard-on straining against his designer jeans. Freaking sponsorships. He hated wearing the uncomfortable style but it paid his most extravagant bills.

Granted, he seemed tame compared to some of the celebrity bad-boy drivers, but he knew how to have a good time when the mood struck. He'd had flashier girls than Lynn throw themselves in his direction, but something special had happened when he spotted her. Older than him, sophisticated, classy and so different from the women he fucked around with—he couldn't stop imagining what she'd look like laid out on his king-sized mattress, wearing only that smirk.

Best of all, she didn't seem to recognize him. The chemistry between them had nothing to do with his money, his racing or the ridiculous hype his marketing department cooked up. Unbelievable. He wasn't about to let her get away unless she'd already been spoken for. He didn't cheat and he'd never sleep with someone else's woman, no matter how bad he wanted to.

Well, without the guy's permission anyway. There had been a few times... His mind conjured a vivid image of Lynn sandwiched between him and his navigator Mark as they ravished her bold curves.

He had to shake his head to clear the ringing in his ears when he realized she'd answered him but he'd missed her response. A woman like her would never be into the nasty games he'd played with the groupies who'd made for an easy feast in his younger years.

"I mean, I've been in relationships of course." He grinned when a blush stained her cheeks. She grimaced then sputtered, "Just not at the moment."

"Nice. Then I don't have to worry about someone hunting me down for buying you dinner." He adjusted his cock as discreetly as he could when he sat, but the confining jeans wouldn't hide his obvious arousal if she so much as glanced at his crotch again.

She groaned. "Don't tease. There's nothing open in this hellhole, is there?"

"Nope. The lone McDonald's is on the other side of the security checkpoint. They're not letting anyone through. But your stomach's growling loud enough I thought I was on a safari. So, I brought you a three-course vending machine banquet." Sebastian hoped she wasn't too prissy to pig out on junk food with him. He hadn't needed to worry.

"Please tell me you scored some of those tiny powdered donuts."

"You'll have to wait and see. First up, the amuse-bouche." He handed her a bottle of water before he presented a bite-sized caramel with a flourish.

"I think I love you," she sighed.

When she reached to take the morsel from his hand, he withdrew. "Uh-uh. This is a fixed menu for two."

He unwrapped the candy then held it between his fingertips a few inches in front of her mouth. Lynn rolled her eyes then accepted his silent dare instead of telling him to fuck off. She leaned forward until her exposed cleavage had his mouth watering then wrapped her lips around the treat and bit it in half. A thin line of caramel stretched. It broke, leaving a sweet trail at the corner of her mouth.

Sebastian would have given the entire payout of his next race to lick it off but he'd pushed his luck enough already. He swiped the gooey mess from her lips then brought his thumb to his tongue along with the other half of the caramel. The flavor of her skin surpassed the sweetness of the candy.

"Mmm, delicious."

Her regal neck flexed as she swallowed, making it far too easy to imagine her throat working around him instead. He groaned.

"Looks like I'm not the only one with a sweet tooth."

"You have no idea." The rough tone of his voice surprised him. He shook himself, trying to find some restraint. He couldn't bear to frighten her off.

"Next up, the main course. He slid the bundled beef jerky and cheddar cheese from his pocket then offered it to her. When he ripped open the packaging, a loud gurgle drowned out the crinkle of plastic. "Damn, no screwing around. You're really hungry. It sucks that they've cut all the snacks out of your domestic flights."

She didn't argue, accepting the meager offering with a murmured, "Thanks."

After she chewed and swallowed a hunk of dried meat, she asked, "Is there still a land of free munchies? Where are you from?"

"A tiny village on the Amalfi Coast."

"Which one?" She popped another nugget into her mouth. Such contrasts. An all-business skirt and blouse in dove gray and pink matched her perfect French manicure but couldn't detract from the hints of wicked mischief flashing in her eyes or her ability to enjoy the simple pleasures he'd brought her.

"Oh, nowhere you'd know."

"Try me." Her arched eyebrow made him sorry to squash her rebelliousness when he proved her wrong.

"Erchie."

"Ah, yes. Often overlooked. Closer to Salerno than Sorrento.

It's actually one of the stops on my itinerary."

"You're kidding! What are you planning to do there?"

"Write travel guides. For women. Alone." She blushed then studied the tiles as though embarrassed for not having a companion. "At least I hope to. I quit my job to give it a go."

"No shit. You'll have to stay at my mother's bed and breakfast. The rooms are small but cozy and she cooks the best pasta in all of Italy. She'd make any *ragazza* feel right at home as long as they don't mind her talking their ears off or going into town to gossip with her friends."

"That sounds perfect." Her smile lit up the gloomy terminal. "But I'm sure she'll be booked solid this time of year."

"You can have my old room. She refuses to rent it out in case I'm able to make it home in between events. Like I'd mind crashing on the couch for a night or two. But she won't hear of it." He chucked as he thought of the horror on his mother's face when he'd proposed the idea last.

Truth was, though he'd spent his youth ticking off the days until he could escape his lazy village to someplace urban and fast-paced, lately he longed for the peace he'd known while lounging on the beach, swimming in the jewel blue waters of the Mediterranean or fishing with his father before he'd lost his battle with cancer. "Depending on the timing, maybe I could meet you there."

The thought of this woman in his boyhood bed had his molars throbbing as he ground them to dust. It only got worse when she licked salt from her fingertips, one by one.

"I couldn't ask you to do that." She chuckled.

As though it would be any kind of imposition.

"What events were you talking about? What do *you* do?"

"Ah. I drive." He relished the dilation of her pupils when he revealed the pack of donuts he'd stashed behind his back, feeling only a little guilty for distracting her. He didn't want to ruin their casual exchange. People always got weird when they found out. "Dessert?"

"Oh yeah. I never pass it up. If you couldn't tell." She nibbled one side of the cake ring he shared, paying no mind to the powdered sugar snowing onto her clothes.

"Me either."

Her gaze snapped to his, searing him with her green laser stare for several moments before she steered the conversation to her original goal. “So…you drive. A taxi?”

“Not exactly.”

“Then what, exactly?” She refused to surrender. He loved that.

“Rally cars.” He shrugged, hoping to play it off. It didn’t mean as much in the States where the sport had never grown popular.

“Wow! A racecar driver.”

Sebastian tamped down the pride attempting to flair at the approval in her voice.

“That can’t be an easy thing to pursue. I mean, doesn’t every boy dream of speed? I wish I’d refused to give in to reality when I was your age.”

He laughed out loud. “My age! *Dio*, you make it sound like you’re a hundred years old. Bust out the ‘whippersnapper’ or maybe ‘kids today’, why don’t you?”

“Come on, you’re what…twenty-five?”

“Twenty-eight.”

“I turned forty this year!”

“Though some things get finer with age, it’s still just a number, Lynn.” He studied the pinched corner of her lips. She frowned as she swallowed the final crumbs of the donut. “You’re free now and going after what you want. That’s all that matters.”

He cursed under his breath when he reminded her of their situation. In an instant, she morphed into a bundle of tension.

“What am I doing? I have to get out of here. I need to make it to New York.” She glanced at her watch then checked the board once more as though expecting a miracle. “There’s no way I’ll make it if I wait for the flight. Will you watch my things for a minute?”

“Can I peek at *your* underwear?”

“Hell no!” A chuckle broke from her as she pressed a palm to her cheek. She began to turn then came closer instead. “I don’t wear any.”

Her scandalous whisper reverberated through his chest straight to his straining erection as he watched her float away. Her unpracticed flirting turned him on more than the skilled seduction he'd enjoyed from women in the past. He couldn't take his eyes off her as she sashayed toward the counter where the line had died down some.

Sebastian didn't notice the hyper child running past until it was too late. The kid skipped from black tile to black tile, lassoing his ankle in Lynn's purse strap. Tangled, the child and the bag crashed to the floor. Sebastian reached out to make sure the boy hadn't hurt himself but the child's mortified mother beat him to it. When she'd assured herself the kid was fine, she started a lecture on public behavior with, "Tommy John Andrews..."

Ouch! He'd always hated it when he earned a full-name reprimand.

With a wink at the boy, he gathered the scattered contents of Lynn's carry-on. He set her netbook on the bench then reached for the books that had tumbled free. The graphic covers had him doing a double take.

Holy shit! That couldn't be what it looked like.

Yet, sure enough, when he scooted the first one closer for a thorough inspection, he confirmed the *two* men depicted both had their hands beneath the skirt of the women between them.

His pulse spiked, maybe even skipped a beat here and there. The thick paper swished as he thumbed through the novel, picking out juicy scenes to browse. Lynn moved up from gorgeous, sweet and funny to his dream woman in a matter of seconds.

Passionate possibilities flooded his mind. Had she ever tried ménage? Bondage? Or even the raw, primal sex for two filling the pages in his hands? He doubted it. Hell, the woman had nearly choked on a tiny tease over going commando.

He would love to show her all she had missed.

When her netbook dinged from near his ear as he crouched on the floor, he jerked hard enough to bang his knee under the seat. "Sorry," he mumbled to the grouchy man he'd jarred from a nap.

Guilty much, Fiori?

The flashing icon in the system tray caught his attention. His finger moved toward the touchpad despite his attempt to restrain himself. Shit, that'd never been his strong suit.

The new email contained a link to comments on a blog. He

clicked before his conscience could catch up with his caveman instincts.

Tempt The Cougar. He didn't realize he'd started grinning like a madman until his cheeks ached. His gorgeous crush hid more than she let on. So she thought he was sexy? Good to know.

Sebastian scanned the posts. He must have done something really, really good—like saving the planet good—in a previous life. Lynn and her friends were into younger men. How about that?

Sam: Do it, Lynn! Or, should I say, do him?

Autumn: Ohhh, does he have any cute friends?

Stevie: Sneak us a pic with your phone!

Larissa: Back off, Cougars. You all have studs of your own. I understand being cautious, Lynn, but there's a difference between that and isolation. If you can, see where it goes. It's okay to have fun every once in a while. Rawrrrr!

LynnLuvs2Trvl: Hey, ladies. Lynn stepped away for a minute. I promise I'm not a serial killer. Your friend is beautiful. The attraction is not one-sided. You can check me out. My name is Sebastian Fiori. I'm a rally car driver for Driven Wild. Go ahead, Google me. I can give you references…'cause I'm telling you now, I'm interested in fulfilling her fantasies. Maybe you could put in a good word for me?

Darci: Holy crap! She wasn't joking. You're HOT!

LynnLuvs2Trvl: Uh, thanks.

Rachel: If you hurt her, we will hunt you down. My fiancé is a cop.

LynnLuvs2Trvl: She's safe with me. I swear it. She'll call you when we get to NY. Give me four hours before you release the hounds.

Rachel: How are you going to get there?

LynnLuvs2Trvl: I have a plan, don't worry.

Chapter Three

"Excuse me. I realize you're swamped right now but I have a flight to Europe to catch in less than five hours. Can you give me any estimate at all of how long it might be before we're en route?"

"Sorry, ma'am." The freckle-faced kid made her feel ancient. "I'm not supposed to say."

No use in hassling the guy. She'd worked her share of shit jobs in her college years. "I understand. Thanks, anyway."

Just as she turned, the kid whispered, "But…if I were you, I'd go for a rental car. With this mess, you'll be lucky to snag one. If you can though, the drive's only four hours or so. If traffic's not bad, you'll make your flight. That's more than I can promise if you hang around here."

Lynn nodded. "That's what I thought."

"Let me call for you. I have the number on speed dial." He tapped the monstrous phone on his desk then waited a beat before asking, "Hey, Russell, can I make a reservation for a passenger? I'm going to send her right over to you."

She held her breath as the kid listened. Then sighed when he cursed under his breath.

"Nothing at all? Not even to carpool up to JFK?" Another pause. "Yeah, trust me, you should see things in here. It's a zoo today. I don't get paid enough for this. Not your fault, man. Thanks."

He didn't meet her gaze as he replaced the handset in the cradle as though he expected her to rant and rave.

"It's okay. I appreciate you trying." Lynn couldn't prevent her disappointment from shading her tone.

"Want me to see what's available for standby, maybe we can reroute you?"

"There's not enough time…"

Lynn jumped when someone cupped her elbow. Without looking, she recognized Sebastian's scent and the gentle yet firm way he ensnared her. She leaned into his hold as her knees turned to jelly.

"That won't be necessary. I've made other arrangements for us."

"You did what?" Her hackles rose. She hadn't fought to break every single confining influence in her life only to let some stranger start making her decisions.

He ignored her outrage. "Could you please have our luggage forwarded to our final destination?"

Sebastian passed a torn corner of paper with an address scribbled on it over her head. She concentrated on closing her gaping mouth and relaxing her contorted face in case it stuck like that. As if she needed more wrinkles!

"Yes of course, Mr. Fiori."

She whipped around to face the attendant. Obviously rally car racing meant more than she'd realized. Her young coconspirator stared at Sebastian as she imagined he would Superman or maybe one of the Yankees.

"How do you know where I'm headed?" The squeak came out an octave above her usual tone.

"Your friends told me you're starting your trip in Paris. I'm on my way to France for a rally. By the way, Rachel says to have a good time." He had the balls to wink at her.

She sputtered, trying to find the anger she knew should raise her blood pressure over his violation of her privacy. Still, none seemed to materialize. Had he opened the door to her fantasies? Could it be so horrible to accept his offer if it was what she would have chosen anyway?

At least she didn't have to face humiliation. When he'd discovered the blog, he could have left—could have walked away without looking over his shoulder. But he hadn't. He'd come to claim her.

"I'd love to get to know you better." His knuckles skimmed her cheekbone, sending a rush of anticipation through her. "Besides, it's the only way you're going to make it on time. I promise not to bite. Unless you ask nice."

Before self-doubt sabotaged her instincts, she nuzzled his fingers then turned her face to nip one. "Let's go then. Don't want to miss our flight."

She'd forgotten about their audience until the young man cleared his throat. "C-could I get your autograph?"

"Sure. What's your name?" Sebastian worked a silver Sharpie and a glossy collector card from his back pocket.

"Jim."

Holy crap. He'd come prepared. She gawked at the image of him posing in a full-body racing suit. It shouldn't be possible for one man to look that sexy.

Sebastian jotted a quick note then signed the thick stock. "Nice to meet you, Jim. Thanks for taking care of the luggage."

"No problem. This rocks!" The two guys bumped fists, a trend she would never understand. Still, she didn't linger on the generational difference between her and Sebastian. How could she when he made it effortless to stay near him?

They waved as they left the counter. She attempted to unburden Sebastian by reclaiming her carry-on but he refused to let her shoulder it, instead, stacking it on top of his own duffle. When she drifted near the rental car kiosks, he draped an arm around her waist then steered her toward the terminal exit instead.

"You got a car already?"

"I didn't have any luck with the rentals either." He frowned. "We're going to have to let someone else drive."

"What do you mean?" Her eyes narrowed a moment before they made their way outside. "Sebastian! You can't hire a limo for a four-hour drive. It's going to cost a fortune!"

"You want to make our flight, gorgeous?"

She sighed. "Let me pay for half."

"No need." When she would have objected, he silenced her by pressing his lips to hers, catching her off guard. Any possible argument evaporated from her brain as she soaked in the heat of his embrace. Her palms landed on his sculpted chest. His long fingers supported her neck while his lips sampled each of hers then traced the seam between them. She gasped at the sensation, parting for his gentle exploration. Instead of pressing his advantage though, he retreated.

Dazed, she didn't understand him at first when he murmured, "This one's on Driven Wild. They need me there for the time trials. Ride up to New York with me. I want to get to know you better."

She wondered exactly what he had in mind when his palms skimmed over her shoulder then along the length of her back until he stopped a fraction of an inch short of her ass. The old Lynn would have waited to see what developed. The new Lynn didn't have that kind of patience.

No more wasted time, remember? "Does getting to know each other involve talking or making out?"

She bit her lip as she hoped he understood she couldn't quite go for broke yet. What she really wanted to ask was, "Are we going to get it on in the limo?"

What would she do if he expected them to mess around? Would she run toward the waiting car or away from it? She couldn't say for certain, but she knew which option her soaked pussy voted for.

"I'm yours for the ride, gorgeous. Whatever you like, I'm here to please. No pressure either way. No judgment and no hard feelings."

The chauffer rounded the car then held the gleaming door open as they hashed out the details of their arrangement. Sebastian inched forward, nudging her toward the waiting vehicle. She'd never faced temptation so strong before. Not one reason to refuse him came to mind.

Lynn surrendered. Her forehead rested on his chest as she agreed, "Let's go."

"You won't regret it."

Lynn smiled across the intimate space at Sebastian as he described growing up in one of the most beautiful places on earth. Eyes closed, he tipped his head into the rest. His legs splayed on the supple leather bench seat. An empty flute held the remnants of the champagne they'd split. Though it hadn't yet been an hour since they'd left Harrisburg, the steady clip of miles rolling by felt like sand pouring through an hourglass.

Their legs pressed together from knees to feet. They'd both kicked off their shoes once they'd settled into the plush limo. His socked toes rubbed against hers then up to her ankle idly as they talked, hopping from subject to subject.

Considering their age differences, they had an amazing amount in common.

"What's your favorite food?"

She blinked while her mind caught up to what he'd asked. "I love spaghetti."

"Me too," he grinned. "It's sort of required by my birthright."

"White wine or red?" she countered.

"Red all the way."

"I agree." She smiled.

A horn blast jolted her from their exchange. Sebastian cursed then peered out the window as streams of traffic passed them on the left. The knuckles of his hand turned white where they rested on his knee.

"It really does bother you not to drive, doesn't it?" Lynn covered his fingers with her own, loosening their grip. God, his hands were huge compared to hers. So strong.

"Stupid, right?" He shook his head in chagrin.

"No, not when you're so highly trained. I can understand how it would make you anxious." She massaged his ultra-tense thigh muscle until he relaxed a smidge.

"If I were up there, I could get us to New York in two hours flat."

"But then we'd have less time for…this."

He leaned forward, resting his elbows on his knees until she couldn't evade his piercing gaze. "Distract me?"

"How?" Lynn gulped.

"Come sit here while we talk." He patted the seat beside his hip.

Tired of tiptoeing around the chemistry threatening to blow them both to smithereens, she did one better. She crawled onto his lap. He smiled as he reached for her. The bulk of his shoulders filled her arms when she wrapped them around him before letting him tug her the rest of the way over him. Soft fabric teased her thighs as her skirt rode higher. She settled, kneeling with one leg on either side of his trim hips.

Sebastian shifted forward to give her room to explore the broad expanse of his back with her greedy hands. His abdomen fit tight against her. The pressure of his hard-on imprinting on her belly had her sucking in a breath. The expansion of her chest melded her hard nipples to his solid pecs. She squirmed beneath the weight of her arousal, hoping to get it under control.

No such luck. She moaned aloud.

"You're so responsive. That's such a turn-on." He stroked her hair, making her glad she'd taken the extra time to blow-dry and curl it with her fat, round brush before packing the last of her toiletries this morning. Somehow it had felt like a special occasion. "And so gorgeous."

"And almost twice your age. Do you go for older women often?"

"Never before you. You're everything I was looking for but didn't know I wanted. It's not a pick-up line or something. You're so damn refined compared to the women I've dated. But not stuck-up or snobby. More like…graceful, elegant, mature and reserved."

His genuine awe erased her self-consciousness.

No answer came to mind when his full lips mesmerized her. She swore the flavor of him from the airport lingered, mingling with the champagne they'd drunk. Delicious. She craved another taste.

The greenish-blue of his eyes reminded her of the Mediterranean waters he'd described with heartfelt sentiment, rivaling the greatest poetry she'd ever read. With the addition of the heat in them, she half expected them to steam up.

Unable to resist a moment longer, she buried her fingers in the unruly locks of his thick brown hair then captured his mouth. This kiss held no hint of the gentle coercion they'd shared earlier. No, this time she pillaged, taking what she wanted while he gave as good in return.

Euphoria washed over her, urging her to ride the wave. For the first time in her life, she understood what the word "lust" really meant. When she ground her pelvis into his, he met the motion with a thrust of his own, stroking her aching core with his denim-encased hard-on.

That's when she heard the *whhhhp* of something ripping.

"Oh my God. Did I hurt you?" She would have scrambled off him but he still had one arm wrapped around her.

Instead of shrieking in pain, he laughed. And laughed. And laughed.

"What's so funny?"

When he collapsed against the seat, leaving a wedge of space between their torsos, she saw it too. Lynn slid to the floor between his knees to get a better look at the split seam in the crotch of his jeans.

"Fucking sponsors. These damn things were about to castrate me."

Afraid her eyes might bulge out of her skull, she couldn't help herself. She traced the frayed edge of the hole—where his olive flesh peeked from beneath the confining packaging—with the tip of her index finger.

"You're not wearing underwear either," she whispered.

"Never do," he growled behind clenched teeth. "I'm getting rid of these before the button gives way and puts your eye out. Safety first, gorgeous."

"Let me." She brushed his hands away from her target. When their fingers skimmed his erection, he hissed.

"Hurry."

Lynn shoved his gray t-shirt up his six-pack abs to expose the waistband of his jeans. She wrestled the button at the top of his fly. It gave way, tearing the zipper open as well.

"Ahhh." Sebastian groaned as she relieved the pressure on his straining cock.

He had her previous lovers beat by a solid three inches. Her mouth watered at the sight.

Together they peeled his jeans from his hips. He lifted to help her strip them off then sat, unashamed and primed, before her. She peeked up at his face from her place on the floor, her lashes lowered.

"Whatever you want," he murmured.

"I want you."

CHAPTER FOUR

Lynn licked a trail from Sebastian's knee along his thigh. She nipped the ridge of muscle in his quad. While she slaked the urges drowning out every practical facet of her nature, she watched him shuck his shirt in her peripheral vision.

The man was in his prime, no doubt about that.

She reached up to trace the contours of his abdomen as it flexed in time with his uneven respiration. Still, he didn't goad her or make any move to take control.

The freedom to explore, to do as she pleased, had her heart racing almost as much as the attraction rushing through her veins. A wicked impulse prodded her to tease him further before rewarding his patience.

Scant inches from his erection, she turned her head to let her breath wash over his balls. Then she rocked onto her haunches. Sebastian's hands fisted on the seat beside his thighs. True to his word though, he didn't pressure her to continue.

"Thank you," she whispered.

Disappointment dulled the hunger in his eyes though he tried to hide it with a half-hearted smile. When she spun around, coming to her feet with her hands braced on the opposite seat, his stare blazed once more. Tapping a reservoir of brazen sensuality she hadn't known she possessed, she rocked from side to side, causing her skirt to flash glimpses of her bare ass and pussy, if the cool breeze was any indication.

Even the chilly air didn't stand a chance at tempering her arousal. The moisture coating her thighs probably glistened in the fancy halogen lighting of the cabin. Hopefully it didn't highlight her flaws as well. If it did, Sebastian didn't seem to mind. He groaned when she tucked her fingers into her stretchy waistband then shimmied until the fabric pooled around her bare toes.

"Gorgeous."

She snuck a glance over her shoulder. His hand had migrated to his crotch where he alternated cupping his balls and stroking his magnificent erection, which seemed to have swollen to greater proportions. She licked her lips when she caught sight of the defined ridges of his veins. They'd feel amazing tunneling inside her.

The low, rock beat filling the car set the perfect rhythm for her striptease.

She spun around then sat, mirroring him on the opposite seat. Her spread legs presented him with her bare pussy.

"You shave," he panted.

"Wax."

He scrunched his eyes closed for a moment as his hand hesitated in its circuit along his hard-on. A feline grin tugged one corner of her mouth upward. Power had her head spinning double-time. Her heavy breasts demanded to be freed from the confines of her bra.

Lynn flicked her fingers over the bottom button on her blouse, releasing it. Then she did the same for the top closure. She worked her way toward the middle, running her hands over her flaming skin to soothe some of her restless energy but only ended up escalating the frenzy of desire burning within her.

She continued until one single point held her shirt closed over her chest.

"You're killing me."

"Me too," she rasped as she approached him once more. She bent over so his face nestled in her cleavage. The coarse stubble of his sparse shadow rasped the soft mounds of her breasts.

"Undo it," she demanded. When his hands wandered up her sides toward his goal, she covered them with her own, squeezing gently. "No, with your teeth."

Sebastian complied. He latched on then yanked the panel until the button flew off. Then he licked and bit her breast as he rooted around the edge of the lace cups, working her nipple free.

Wet heat surrounded the hardened tip as he drew on it with lazy pulls of his lips. His tongue flicked over the flushed peak, causing her toes to curl in the carpet. He devoured her with honest yearning so intense it stole her breath.

Lynn shrugged out of the blouse then reached behind her back. She unclasped her bra, letting it fall to the floor. The hand she braced on his shoulder steadied her while she indulged his appetite, allowing him to feast on her breasts until she saw stars. Her thighs rubbed each other as she attempted to relieve some of the pressure building between her legs.

She needed more. Had to have him touching her.

A slick pop marked the exit of her nipple from his mouth when she retreated to the seat behind her. She propped her legs up, exposing herself completely to the young, virile man before her. Her heels sank into the cushion.

He didn't need her to spell out her wishes. Goose bumps rose on her arms when he made a predatory lunge toward her. Agile, fit and determined, he stole her breath.

The span of his long fingers cupped her thighs as he pushed them higher and farther apart to make room for his broad shoulders. Without a moment's hesitation, he buried his face in her soaked pussy.

"*Dio*, you're so hot. *Molto dolce, bella.*" She didn't speak Italian but she understood the language of his touch, the urgency in his tone as he mumbled against her swollen flesh. The vibration of his praise added to the ecstasy of his manipulation.

His tongue traced the rim of her opening as his lips sipped the dew from her labia, working steadily upward toward her clit. Her fingers clenched on his shoulders and back, urging him closer. Desperation drove her to rake her nails over him, forcing him to take more, but he didn't seem to mind. Instead, he redoubled his efforts, losing the hint of playfulness he'd had before.

A moan escaped her chest when his teeth skimmed her sensitive skin. He positioned one of her thighs on his shoulder as his hand journeyed inward toward her throbbing pussy.

"Yes! Sink your fingers in me. I want to be filled." The stark honesty of her expressed desires startled her. Sex had never been this good—this raw or this powerful—for her. He allowed her to fulfill the sensual potential she'd given up on reaching.

The tip of one finger swirled through the juices streaming from her as he concentrated the flicks of his tongue on the area surrounding her clit. The indirect stimulation eased her into the full-on pressure of his lips.

Fireworks exploded in brilliant shades of red and gold behind her clamped eyelids. She forced herself to open them so she didn't miss a moment of Sebastian's expert seduction.

He worked his digit inside her by degrees until the knuckles of his other fingers settled into the valley of her ass. Pleasure tightened every muscle of her body, causing her to hug his embedded hand. The ripple of her channel around him elicited a moan from each of them.

Shocks of bliss fizzled up her spine as he moved within her. Each wiggle of his tongue on her clit pushed her higher. She couldn't stand to toe the edge of orgasm much longer. The surfeit of rapture would drive her insane.

Lynn gripped his hair in her fist, aligning him with the one spot sure to set her off in seconds. "Make me come, Bastian. Now."

He growled as he delved deeper, his finger rotating to press her G-spot against her pelvic bone. Then his lips surrounded her clit, his mouth doing something magical to her pussy. She fucked his face without restraint. He followed the arc of her hips with enthusiastic laps of his tongue.

The flex of her pussy around him forced more lubrication onto his hand. He groaned when it eased his way, allowing him to sink a little deeper. The echo of his praise for her uninhibited display shattered her. Spasm after spasm threatened to rip her apart.

When she thought the climax couldn't get any stronger, he rubbed the rough patch inside her, renewing her orgasm. She screamed his name as he continued to eat her, wringing every last drop of passion from her.

He read the slowing of her contractions, bringing her down easy from dizzying heights. No man had ever been so in tune with her body. Boneless, she sagged in his supporting grasp, attempting to catch her breath.

"Gorgeous," he whispered in between butterfly kisses on her thigh, mons and stomach.

She couldn't summon the energy to move, though kneeling on the floor had to be uncomfortable for him. "Hold me?"

Lynn didn't have to ask twice. Sebastian scooped her into his arms then twisted so he rolled onto the seat on his side. She curled into his chest, their legs scissored. The glimmer of her pleasure on his lips enticed her to lick it off. She sampled the arousal he'd inspired when she fused their mouths together. One part him, one part her—the recipe made for a scrumptious result.

Despite the hard-on branding her hip, he attempted gentleness. He caressed her jaw while he nibbled her lips. But sexual tension radiated from him. If she didn't plan to restrain her desires, why should he have to?

Months of abstinence ensured her lust couldn't be wiped away by the initial relief her monumental orgasm had provided. Not with the promise of more arcing between them.

"Do you have any condoms with you?" she whispered, nearly begging.

"There's a whole box in my bag."

"Get them."

While he rummaged through the duffle on the floor beside his head with one hand, he asked, "What's your favorite position, *tesoro*?"

"You ask a lot of questions."

"Want me to find out some other way?" The fingers of his free hand splayed across the small of her back, his thumb tucked under her hipbone. "I could investigate."

"I'm more interested in you. What do you like?"

"Anything. Everything. It depends on the moment, the woman and my mood. Right now, I'd love for you to ride me. I want to watch your tits bounce while you fuck me. The liberation shining in your eyes is addictive. Sexy."

Lynn grabbed the condom he proffered. She moved to the edge of the seat so he could flip to his back. The foil wrapper tore easily when she held one corner between her teeth. Before covering his shaft, she bent to sample the pearly liquid beading in the slit on the head of his penis. She would have taken him in her mouth, savored his heat and musk, but Sebastian edged away.

"Not this time. I won't last." He wrapped his fingers around her wrist then guided the condom closer. "Cover me."

She did as he asked. The thin latex rolled over his cock with some effort. Her hands stroked his length, marveling at the solid mass of his erection. She could play with him all day. But when she caught sight of his agonized face, she realized how much she'd tortured him already.

The bunched muscles of his thigh flexed against the inside of hers when she swung her other leg over his waist. Tipping forward, she plastered them together, chest to chest and pelvis to pelvis. They both gasped at the full-body contact.

Sebastian's arms came around her, his hands wandering to her ass. He grabbed the cheeks, his fingers sinking in as he spread them. She slid her hips forward then back, stroking his length with the wet lips of her pussy. The head of his erection nudged her clit when it jerked beneath her in time to his pounding heart.

She planted her hands on his chest as she humped him shamelessly, lowering her lips to his for a scorching kiss. On each pass, she increased the swing of her hips until the tip of his cock lodged inside the mouth of her pussy, on the cusp of entering.

The pressure had her sighing, anticipating the moment when his penetration would burn her as he stretched her wide.

"Take me inside you," he growled.

They moved at the same time, she rocked her hips up and back while he thrust from below. The head of his cock parted her slick flesh, joining them for the first time. The universe seemed to stop as their eyes met and held.

Sebastian smiled. Then he wrapped his hands over her shoulders and tugged her toward him. Lynn moved in tandem, fitting them together, inch by inch. When he'd made it about halfway, she kissed the exposed sinew of his throat before lifting her torso upright. Her ass rested on her heels as her hands fell back, one on each of his tense thighs. She locked her elbows, using gravity to shove him into her the rest of the way.

When he packed her full, she paused, staring into the depths of his eyes, trying to catch her breath while bands of desire constricted her chest. Had anything ever felt this good?

"Gorgeous, *tesoro*." His hands cupped her presented breasts, thrust forward by her position. "You fit me perfectly."

His cock felt so hot inside her, setting off mini explosions in her abdomen. She bucked, trying to soothe the arousal but only amplified it instead. He impaled her, every nerve ending in her pussy aware of his presence. The contours formed by the ridge of the head and his veined shaft rippled over the spongy walls.

Every rock of her hips dragged her clit across the pad of muscle above his cock.

"That's it. Fuck me." He pinched her nipples, rolling them between his thumb and forefingers. "Ride me hard."

He made it so easy to take what she wanted. Lynn found herself bobbing on him, pounding his length inside her as deep as he could reach. She leaned farther back until the head of his cock nudged her just right every time she forced it through the constricting rings of muscle at her entrance.

Close now, she fucked with less accuracy and more passion. Their bodies expanded and contracted to keep him lodged inside her. Every time the head of his cock locked with the mouth of her pussy, she moaned then relished the long glide of him coming home.

Each muscle in his body tensed, quivering. His sweat-slicked chest, his amazing abs, even the thighs she clenched in her death grip, gathered. Knowing she affected him—that she could stretch him on a rack of desire as inescapable as the one she found herself bound to—was more than she could bear.

The knot of her clit tapped him as she buried him deep then rocked in quick, shallow arcs.

"Lynn. Damn it." Sebastian fought the pleasure she gave him, but when she added a circular grind of her hips to every stroke, he lost. "Going to come."

His hard-on flared inside her as the first hints of her orgasm bubbled in the depths of her abdomen. Every ounce of pleasure she gifted him returned to her double. She reached behind her back to cup his tight sac, holding his balls in her palm.

He roared with satisfaction at the same time the base of his cock jerked against her fingertips. Imagining the rush of his cum filling the condom he wore—combined with the pressure on her clit and the equipment overflowing her pussy—triggered her orgasm.

Her pussy milked him with rhythmic pulses. The relief she experienced went deeper, felt more substantial, with him inside her. Joining her. The grunts he made and the flex of his cock extended her pleasure until she collapsed, limp, on his chest.

Even then, the occasional aftershock vibrated through them, making them both sigh and moan. Though she couldn't imagine moving a muscle, Sebastian seemed rejuvenated. Unable to lie still, he petted her back, stroked her ass, kissed her cheek and played with her hair.

When his half-hard cock slipped from her, he shifted her to the side to take care of the condom. She didn't realize what he intended until the blast of fresh air pebbled her nipples.

She laughed. "Did you throw that out the window?"

"What else was I supposed to do with it?" He shrugged then grinned. "Hope the people behind us were following at a safe distance."

A cotton undershirt dangled from his fist when he knelt by her side once more. She blushed when he spread her legs to dry her before plucking her skirt off the running board.

"Now you're turning shy on me?" He helped her dress before rummaging in his duffle for a change of clothes.

"It's not every day I meet a young stud then assault him in a limousine."

He had no answer for that. She supposed it might not be so far out of the realm of ordinary for him.

"I wish we had more time to lounge naked together. I would love to hold you. But that might be hard to explain if we were in an accident. My mother would not approve." He winked, some of his earlier lighthearted nature emerging from the haze of sensuality that had obscured it.

Once their appearances had been returned to order, he rejoined her on the seat, snuggling close. Still, she found she couldn't let that nagging thought go. She refused to smother her curiosity a moment longer.

"Have you ever done something like this before?"

"Like what?"

"Fooled around with someone you just met?"

"Yes."

She nodded. "I figured."

"But it was never like this, Lynn. Those times were about scratching an itch with girls who sought a notch on their bedpost—wanted to say they fucked Sebastian Fiori. Not me, my name."

He couldn't obscure the bitterness underlying his resignation.

"If it makes you feel better, you're a no-name to me." She smiled. "Or at least you were. I'll never forget you now."

"Same here, gorgeous." His fingertip traced her brow. "I kind of got the feeling this is some kind of experiment for you. I'm glad I was in the right place at the right time. Luckiest day of my life."

"You think I'd have done this with any hot guy I met?" She started to sit up but he tucked her closer. "Bastian, that's not true. Believe me, I have lots of fantasies. Yes, one of them was to take a younger lover, but I've never wanted to make one come true as much as when I met you."

"Tell me about the books in your purse. Are they about things you want to try? Or simply something to dream about?"

Ridiculous, considering what they'd done, she blushed again. "I guess they're a hot fantasy. Not something I ever expected to experience but something to wonder about. Sort of like winning the lotto. Part of the fun of buying a ticket is imagining what you'd do with the winnings because that's as close as you'll ever get, you know?"

"I suppose." He nuzzled her neck. "I've never bought a lotto ticket. If I want something, I try to figure out how I can get it myself."

Admiration for her lover flared in her chest.

"Someday, I hope I can say the same."

"What if I know a way you can? At least with these…"

"Mr. Fiori, we're nearing JFK. Which gate do you require?" The chauffer buzzed through the tinted glass partition on the intercom.

Lynn's heart bottomed out. Her time with this incredible man had expired. Sure, they'd be on the same plane, but now she had no doubt he'd be flying first class with flight attendants hanging on every request while she suffered through the nine-hour journey squashed in coach. If she got really lucky, she'd be seated between an armrest hogger and someone intent on talking her ear off when all she wanted to do was relive these past four hours, over and over.

"Terminal three, gate eleven," she supplied. At the same time he said, "Terminal four, gate nine."

Oh no! They weren't on the same flight after all. She'd have less than five minutes to say goodbye as the first airport signs zipped past the window.

"Terminal four, please," he repeated for the driver then clicked the channel closed and cleared his throat. "Lynn, I told the airline to release your seat, that you'd made other plans. The flight was oversold even before the weather jacked stuff up. They were looking for any reason to generate free spots."

This time he couldn't hold her when she shoved away from his betraying warmth. "Who the fuck do you think you are? I gave up everything I know for this opportunity. You think you can make decisions for me after knowing me for less than five minutes?"

"Listen, please." He held his hand out, palms facing her when she contemplated chucking her shoe at him. "It's not as bad as you think. I wasn't sure if we were going to make it here on time with the traffic. Look, it's already six forty-five."

She hauled her cell from her purse then dropped her head in her hands. Hormones had distracted her when she could least afford it. He was right. Even if she'd run or found a trolley to drive her, she would have had a hard time making it to her gate before they released her seat for the international flight.

"So why'd you bother with all this nonsense?" She waved at the decadent car. "You were that sure you'd get in my skirt?"

"Not at all."

She crossed her arms over her chest, trying to ignore the husky note to his voice. Like she gave a crap if she'd hurt his pride.

"I made other arrangements for us. I'm sorry, I should have asked but I didn't think you'd accept. Not until you knew me better. I didn't plan for this to happen, but I'd be lying if I said I didn't hope." A ghost of his previous smile returned. "I still think you're gorgeous."

Anger at his ability to melt her insides, even now, had her snapping at him. "Cut that out. Tell me how I'm getting to Europe."

"On the team's private jet."

Had she heard him right? "Private jet?"

"Uh, yeah. I came to the States with my navigator Mark. We checked out a few brake suppliers we're considering changing to. After that, he went to visit some family while I did a little sightseeing. I was meeting him here for the flight to France."

"You're making a transatlantic flight on a private jet." She couldn't stop herself from repeating herself even though she knew she sounded ridiculous.

"Yep." He grinned. "Are you impressed yet? I'm kind of banking on that, you know?"

"Holy crap." She shook her head. "And you're sure it's okay for me to come along?"

"I cleared it with our owner. And Mark." His lids grew heavy as he stared at her, the embers of their lust glowing a little brighter for a moment. "He's looking forward to meeting you."

"What did you tell him about me?" Suspicion had her pulse picking up speed with every beat of her heart.

"Enough." Sebastian scrubbed his hand through his hair before settling her onto his lap once more. Shock numbed her too much to fight. Besides, his touch calmed even when it should have repulsed. "If you just need a lift, we're more than glad to help. If you want to check out the private cabin with me, that's even better. And if you want to reach for your fantasies, win the lotto…well, you're holding the ticket. All you have to do is cash it."

She couldn't deny the pressure of his cock, hard once more, against her thigh.

"You'd be okay with that? Sharing me with your friend?" Part of her became horny as hell as she considered the possibility, but part of her cried that he didn't want to keep her for himself. Stupid, considering they'd met mere hours ago. How could she think their affair could be more than a simple fuck?

"I'm not going to lie, *tesoro*. I've done it before. But…" He shook his head. "It's fine. If that's what you want, it's fine. More than fine." His fingers clenched on her hip and knee.

"How much time do we have before take off? When do I have to decide?"

"It's not an ultimatum. Fly with me. See what develops, okay?"

They pulled up to the curb as he pressed a gentle kiss to her lips. She nodded but she already suspected their voyage could have only one destination. It wasn't every day someone held a golden ticket.

What a waste it would be not to use it.

Chapter Five

The driver opened the door then handed her out. Was it too much to hope for an internet connection in the terminal?

"We have to be on board in twenty minutes. I'm going to check on our luggage. Why don't you call Rachel and let her know you're okay? I'm a little afraid of your friends." He joked but she caught the serious kernel in his eyes.

He'd lobbed her a perfect excuse to get some advice and she would grab it.

"Thank you." She hugged him tight. Maybe he'd gone about things all wrong, but she could admit to herself that she'd have been royally screwed—and not the fun kind—if he hadn't done it. "I'll meet you at the gate in fifteen minutes."

Lynn found a bench in a quiet corner. This terminal had a much classier feel than the cramped, utilitarian commercial wings. Her finger tapped the icon for Rachel in her contact list. Unsure if the thing had even rung, her best friend's shriek almost destroyed her eardrum.

"Tell me everything! Are you okay? What's going on?" In the background she thought she heard Ethan trying to calm his fiancée.

"I'm good. Everything's good. Great really." She hesitated.

"Are you sure?" Rachel pressed.

"Yes." The aura of her sexual conquest had been tainted by her doubts. "It's just…well, Sebastian has a bad habit of acting before asking. He's done it twice in the nanosecond I've known him."

"Did he hurt you?" The *shwing* of her friend's claws coming out rang through the line.

"No, that's not it. But he trampled my pathetic attempt at being in charge of my destiny."

"That's the price you pay for having a hotheaded, younger man in your life. You just met. He doesn't understand what you've been through yet. But there are definite bennies too. Speaking of…did you fuck him?"

"Rach!" Ethan's outrage traveled over the line.

"Uh…"

"You did! I knew it! God, he's smoking. And really good at his job. I researched him for you. He's won the title in his class the last three years in a row."

Why should Lynn feel any measure of pride over that? It wasn't as if she'd had a hand in it. Still, something inside her glowed for him.

"I only have a few minutes, Rach. I'm flying to France with him on his team's private jet."

"Holy shit! He's hot, successful, good in bed *and* he has access to a private jet? You bitch!"

Ethan mumbled in the background. Something about the *Kama Sutra*.

Lynn really didn't want to know.

"I never said he was good in bed." She'd burn in hell for implying he wasn't.

"Whatever! I can hear it in your voice. Okay, okay, I'm under control now. What the heck do you need me for? Sounds like you've got things well in hand."

"He…" She had to stop and clear her throat before starting again. "He found my books. There's going to be another guy with us. His navigator. Sebastian implied they're into *ménage*."

Nothing came across the line.

"Hello?" She peered at the display on her cell, which claimed to still be connected. Not now! She banged the thing against the heel of her palm. "Rachel? Can you hear me?"

"Sorry. Still here. Just… Whoa."

In all the years they'd known each other, Rachel had never

been at a loss for words before.

"Is that a good 'whoa'? Or a bad 'whoa'?" Panic started to breed self-doubt.

"It's a just-wait-until-I-post-this-on-the-blog whoa. I know you, Lynn. If you didn't feel it you would have kicked him to the curb already. The fact you're considering means you really have something going. To be honest, I'm more concerned about that. What are you going to do after tonight? Are you going to be able to walk without getting hurt?"

"I—I don't know. It might be too late for that already." She wished she could put the world on hold to think things through. Then again, hadn't that always gotten her in trouble? Maybe it was time to let go and trust her instincts. "I think I'm going to do it, Rach. If there's a spark between us, I'm going to go for it. I'll figure the rest out later."

"Good for you. Enjoy yourself. Email me when you can so I know you're all right."

"I will. Thanks." She closed her phone with a snap. The digital clock on the front reminded her no more than five minutes of her reprieve remained. No way in hell would she meet Sebastian's friend looking like a something that'd been strapped to the hood of their racecar for a dozen rough miles.

She hustled to the restroom to freshen up.

* * * * *

"Dude. Quit pacing, you're driving me nuts."

Sebastian glared at Mark, the ungrateful bastard. Didn't he realize how much they stood to lose? Letting Lynn out of his sight had been a gamble, but he'd nearly pushed her too far by rearranging her schedule. Maybe she'd tell them to fuck off. "What if she doesn't show?"

"She'll come. You said this trip is important to her, right? There's no other choice today. I came through the main hall from my connecting flight. It's wall-to-wall in there."

He didn't dare tell his friend how bad he hoped Lynn returned because of him—the hell with the lack of alternates. He'd never live that down. At least not until the man had met her. Sebastian found it hard to believe anyone could resist Lynn. How she'd made it this long without some guy claiming her boggled his mind. Unless she didn't want to be tied down.

"Hot damn, is *that* your lady?" Mark looked like a kid in a candy store as he watched Lynn approach.

"Uh-huh." She had gotten even more gorgeous in the past half-hour. He'd swear to it.

"Good eye, Fiori."

"It's more than that, asshole." He regretted the fire in the rebuke when his friend turned to face him, eyebrows raised. Maybe this hadn't been one of his best ideas.

Too late to rescind his offer—not that he'd deny Lynn a chance to explore her fantasy—he reached out to buss her cheeks before making introductions.

He ignored the urge to snatch her away as she hugged Mark in greeting. When her luscious breasts pressed against his friend, she might as well have waved a red flag at the poor sucker. No way could the man resist her stacked frame if given half a chance.

Mark had been his second-in-command since their junior racing days a decade ago. His best friend understood what Sebastian wanted when he lingered instead of clambering onto the plane.

"Very nice to meet you, Lynn. I'll see you two on board. Gotta make a call before we take off." He wore a shit-eating grin as he practically skipped into the Jetway.

"I was afraid you'd run." No use in beating around the bush.

"Me too." She patted his chest then fixed some imaginary wrinkle in his collar before she whispered, "But I couldn't. I would regret it the rest of my life. Not knowing what might have been. I have to say this though. No more stealing my thunder. Only *I* say what goes with me."

"There are no expectations, *tesoro*."

"I'm hardly your treasure." She smiled despite her protest. When she'd translated the term on her phone, his sweetness had caused a warm glow to spread through her.

"Let me be the judge." His thumbs brushed her cheekbones as he bent to kiss her. Long, lingering glides of their lips lulled his anxiety. Everything would be fine as long as she went with him. "Whatever happens…"

He stopped short of promises he didn't think she'd welcome. This should have been a one-night stand. If a fancy one. So why did it feel like the start of a relationship to him instead?

Before he could crack a tooth on his size-eleven sneakers, the flight attendant hailed them from the open door. "Excuse me, Mr. Fiori. The captain is calling for you to board at this time."

"Thanks, Marcy." He nodded to the woman before returning his focus to Lynn. "You ready?"

She grabbed his hand then matched her stride to his as they crossed the threshold in synch. The door locked behind them. There could be no turning back now.

Lynn gasped when confronted with the opulence of the private jet. If the limo had been a giant step up from her Camry, the sleek lounge and dining areas of the aircraft were light years ahead of the standard commuters she'd flown in. Afraid to stain the pure white carpet, she toed off her heels near the entrance.

"Talk about leg room!" A giggle escaped before she could squash it. Unbecoming of a forty-year-old woman, she thought. "I could do cartwheels in here."

"In that skirt, I don't recommend it." Sebastian winked at her.

"Aw, come on. Don't ruin all my fun, *amico*."

She grinned at the easygoing man who'd introduced himself as Mark. A few inches shorter than Sebastian, he had muscles galore. His sandy hair complemented chocolate eyes and olive skin, giving him an appearance that could have come off as boring but definitely did not. His sense of humor sparkled, adding charm to everything he did.

For a situation with a high awkwardness potential, he made her feel right at home.

"But if naked gymnastics are out of the equation there is dinner to look forward to. As soon as we reach cruising altitude. Don't know about you kids but I'm starving. Let's strap in so we can get this show on the road."

The unorthodox seating arrangements threw her. Where exactly did one sit for takeoff? Not in the dining room chairs bolted to the floor, right?

"Join us over here." Sebastian led her to a double lounger, similar to a loveseat. Puffy cushions camouflaged standard airplane seat belts tucked in the seams. They settled onto the chair as Mark claimed the single version, facing them.

The safety spiel played on the huge flat screen at the top of the bulkhead, but all of them had traveled enough to recite it by heart if they chose. Sebastian reached across her waist to grab hold of the buckle then snapped her in. The heat of his touch set her on fire.

For too long, she'd sacrificed her personal life for her career. After two years of clinical orgasms, thanks to her purple, bead-filled, rabbit vibrator, their bout of wild sex had affected her like an alcoholic falling off the wagon. And she was ready to binge.

Lynn didn't realize she and Sebastian had locked gazes until the flight attendant fractured their shared intensity. "All set here?"

"Yes, thanks." Mark answered for them when Sebastian cleared his throat.

"I'll be serving dinner as soon as the captain allows, as you requested. Will you need service before then?" Half Lynn's age, the leggy bombshell made delicious eye candy, but neither Sebastian nor Mark paid the woman much attention.

"If something comes up, we'll ring. Otherwise, go relax up front." Sebastian dismissed the young beauty without looking away from Lynn.

The power of the men's interest had her head swelling by the second.

The engines roared as soon as the woman disappeared behind the curtain separating their space from the galley and crew.

"We've got trivia, movies, some books on the shelf over there and even video games. Seb plays a mean Wii tennis." Mark diffused the tension radiating between them as they inched toward the top of the runway.

"I'm more into the yoga in Fit myself."

"You can actually pull that shit off? Seb and I tried it once but we called it quits when he busted his ass in a lame excuse for the tree pose. Funniest damn thing I've seen." He paused to give his jaw an exaggerated stroke. "Though it might have had something to do with the case of beer we drank before that."

He laughed, the infectious delight drawing a mirroring grin from her.

"*Dio*, you swore you'd never use your powers for evil." Sebastian squeezed her thigh as he gave Mark shit. Unable to resist touching him, she laced their fingers then tipped her head, content to rest against his shoulder, which rocked a bit with his chuckles.

"Tired, *tesoro*?"

"It's been one heck of a day." The engines revved as the captain announced their position as first for departure.

"Damn straight," Sebastian muttered before nudging her chin toward his for a taste of her lips. What seemed like an innocent gesture at first morphed into something serious when neither of them could stop at a tiny peck. They leaned toward each other, angling their faces for better access.

Lynn couldn't say for sure if the concentrated lust of his kiss or the g-force of the jet accelerating down the runway caused her stomach to do more summersaults, but thirty seconds later she soared. She savored the cinnamon flavor of the candy he must have eaten and allowed herself to relax. Despite the short time she'd known him, she realized she trusted him. If she didn't, she never would have gotten on board the plane, or with his plans.

He coaxed her to take his tongue farther into her mouth as he seduced her with broad sweeps of his lips. The perfection of the moment flowed over her, making her dizzy. Her equilibrium shifted as they circled higher and higher above the receding earth. Could she reach for the stars? From here she felt closer than ever before.

She opened her eyes. Sebastian watched her, absorbing every nuance of her reaction. In the limo, she'd acted with pure, desperate need. She'd taken what she wanted. Now she craved something different. Something riskier.

While staring straight into the depths of his stare, as blue and endless as the ocean, she let go of her doubts and fears. She melted into his open arms, allowing him to cradle her exactly as he liked. He might have made fewer revolutions around the sun than she, but he had a hell of a lot more experience than her zilch when it came to no-strings affairs. He could make her burn.

A growl rumbled from his throat. His fingers tensed where they massaged her scalp, mussing her hair.

"So sexy." Mark's smoky timbre startled her. She'd forgotten he existed. Tingles magnified when she thought about the show they put on for him in his front-row seat. "That's right, *cara*. Let Seb take care of you. He will. *We* will, if you let us."

A soft moan betrayed her.

"Watching you make out is getting me hard."

Sebastian couldn't remain unaffected in the wake of Mark's taunting. He nipped her lip then sucked away the sting. Their chests rose and fell with uneven gasps, melding the side of her breast to his forearm in sporadic bursts. She arched, seeking more contact.

"*Seni*, Seb." Mark's foreign direction soothed her universal dilemma when her lover responded, shifting his hand to cup her breast.

His thumb brushed her nipple, coaxing it to tighten beneath his strumming. Grateful for the relief, she snuck a glance in Mark's direction. His dilated pupils fixed on the intersection of Sebastian's skilled fingers and her satin blouse, which covered the heavy globes of her chest. The long, dark lashes surrounding his eyes swept his cheeks with each of his languorous blinks.

One of his hands gripped the armrest hard enough she feared he might bend it. The other cupped the bulge in his pants. His lips parted when he blew out a breath between clenched teeth.

Sebastian relinquished control of her mouth to allow her greater flexibility. She basked in Mark's approval until bursts of ecstasy wrenched her attention to the man feasting on her neck and collarbones. When she reached for her seat belt to free herself, he gripped her wrist.

"Let him play, *cara*." Mark took the devious bastard's side then upped the ante. "Put your hands inside the belt."

When she could force her brain to process his command, she hesitated less than half a second before complying. Sebastian grabbed the free end of the canvas strap and yanked. She squirmed but didn't get far. Her thighs fell open, begging for relief from the pressure he amplified with every touch.

"*Grazioso*. So pretty." Mark groaned when Sebastian worked her skirt up to her waist.

"Let me see *you*, Mark." She froze when the breathy request slipped past her guard. Would it upset Sebastian? She had no idea what to expect. What were the rules here? So unlike anything she'd done before, she hadn't bothered to ask before diving in headfirst, praying Sebastian would be there to catch her.

"I can't," Mark rasped.

She shouldn't have worried. Sebastian paused to grin at her. "You hear that? You're driving him insane, gorgeous. If he puts his hand in his pants right now, he'll come so fast and hard we'll go supersonic."

"He's not the only one." Her head bounced against the rest, her hips rising toward the devious fingertips drawing circles on the inside of her thigh. So close…

"Challenge him, gorgeous. I want to see which of you can hold out longest."

"What's the prize?" The wicked streak she'd embraced grew wider by the moment.

"Winner gets to decide what's for dessert tonight." Sebastian's rough whisper made it clear he had something more decadent than triple-layer chocolate cake in mind.

"Anything they want?" Endless visions of what she'd request—the two men focused on her, both kneeling between her legs, lapping at her soaked pussy, taking turns fucking her into oblivion—overrode her reservations.

"Anything."

"Take your cock out, Mark."

"I love it when you turn bossy." Sebastian nuzzled her jaw.

She smiled. "Me too. Who would have guessed?"

The rustle of Mark shifting for better access drew her attention to him once more. He shoved his t-shirt high on his chest then slid the zipper carefully over the tent in his pants. A rock of his hips accompanied an agile swipe of his hands, which thrust his jeans and boxer briefs to the tops of his thighs. Just low enough to allow his erection to grow upward along his abdomen.

"Impressive." She licked her lips.

"They don't call us Italian stallions for nothing." He winked then grimaced. "But I've got nothing on Seb."

"Mmm." Lynn sighed as she remembered how he'd stretched her. The memory put her in jeopardy of losing their bet before it'd begun. "No fair. That was a low blow."

"Anything goes."

"In that case…wrap your hand around your hard-on. Show me how you jerk yourself off. Long, full strokes from the base to the tip. No skimping."

"Fuck, yes," Mark muttered as he obeyed.

She relished the thrill even as it drove her closer to the end of their match. Arousal bubbled within her, making it hard to catch her breath. Sebastian didn't help any when he walked his fingertips up her thigh to pet her swollen pussy. She gasped.

"Oh yeah, take that." Mark's strained chuckle didn't last long.

"Use your other hand. Play with your balls."

Sebastian looked between them with a grin. "You two aren't screwing around. Good thing, probably twenty minutes or less until Marcy brings dinner. If no one wins before then, *I'm* taking the prize."

"Get your fingers inside her, Fiori. I'll share the reward with you," Mark promised. When Sebastian didn't move quick enough to suit him, he snapped, "Hurry up."

Lynn cried out when her lover's long fingers glided through the ample lubrication dripping from her slit. Three thick digits invaded her clenched rings of muscle until the pad of his palm pressed her clit. "Bastian!"

She attempted to sit still, to keep from writhing on him, but the temptation overpowered her logic. Her hands fisted on either side of her spread thighs, trapped by the strap. Thank God, or she might have yanked Sebastian closer and come on the spot.

"She's so tight. Wait 'til you feel her pussy on your cock. Amazing."

Mark groaned, "Whose side are you on, dude?"

The navigator's hand sped up, making a wet, slapping noise each time he passed over the slick head of his cock.

Instead of answering, Sebastian scissored his fingers inside her, stroking the walls of her pussy until he hit a particularly sensitive spot. She shrieked then trembled, her thighs tensing to try to align his touch once more.

"Oh yeah. Come for him, *cara*." Mark panted. "I can smell your sweetness from here."

"So close." She could surrender now if she wanted. Why didn't she want to again? The promise of a brilliant orgasm weakened her resolve. Rhythmic pulses began to squeeze her around Sebastian, making him work to maintain his pattern of invasion and retreat.

"Me. Too." Mark grimaced. His hand added a twist near the top of his stroke now, rubbing the underside of his cock with the pads of his fingers. His muscles strained, making him look every bit a Roman god straight out of legend. Soon she could have him. Have them both, fucking her together.

Positive she'd lose their challenge in the next moment, Sebastian shocked her by removing his hand from her clit, though he continued to pump his fingers inside her. She cried out as she receded a tiny step from the ledge of ecstasy. With Bastian's hand blocking the view, Mark couldn't tell. Not that he could see well through the slits his eyes had become anyway.

The younger man's hand flew over the straining flesh of his cock for two more seconds before his entire body went stock-still.

"Oh. Fuck," he grunted then his abdomen rippled in a wave of lithe muscle before stream after stream of milky cum poured from the purple tip, glazing his hand, his six-pack and his balls.

The erotic sight had her trembling. Sebastian's fingers slid the fraction of an inch over to the perfect spot he'd abandoned then flexed as he shifted her pleasure into high gear. She bucked against him, rubbing herself shamelessly on his hand. He couldn't deny her now.

The ragged moans echoing from Mark as he wrung satisfaction from every pulse of his orgasm sealed her fate. She exploded, clamping her legs shut to keep Sebastian right where she needed him. Her spine arched, exposing her mouth to him. He didn't waste any time claiming her. The sensual kiss guided her through the tumultuous passion battering her senses until she sagged against the seat, huffing as though she'd run a marathon.

He rubbed their noses together then separated them to bring his drenched digits to his mouth, humming with approval at her taste. When he'd cleaned every last drop of honey from them, he leaned close to whisper in her ear. She hardly heard him over the ringing in them.

"I'm always on your side."

Unsure of how to respond, she stared into the pools of desire in his eyes as he arranged her clothes and released her wrists. The flight attendant saved her from answering when she announced from the doorway, "The captain says you can move freely about the cabin now. I'll have your spaghetti ready in five minutes."

Mark flung aside the pillow he'd used to shield his lap from the woman's view, though she'd have to be a moron to have missed the flush bronzing his skin. He crossed the gap between them then kissed Lynn's cheek. "I gotta get cleaned up first. I'm starving. But don't worry, I'm saving plenty of room for dessert. Nice game."

When he ambled into the restroom near the rear of the plane, she turned to Sebastian with wide eyes.

"*Buon appetito, tesoro.*"

Chapter Six

“That was delicious.” Lynn folded her hands over the linen napkin in her lap. “I still can’t believe you arranged my favorite meal on such short notice.”

“I’m glad you enjoyed it.” Sebastian smiled as he sipped the last of his wine. They’d finished eating over half an hour ago but none of them had budged from the frosted glass table where they shared great conversation and lots of laughs.

Mark had regaled her with stories of their adventures over the past ten years on the circuit. Though he’d probably edited out the worst of the tales, she couldn’t believe some of the things the two of them had been through together. It made her realize how much she’d lost out on while dedicating herself to climbing the corporate ladder.

“What’s that look all about?” Sebastian nudged the base of her chair so the seat swiveled in his direction from her position between the two men.

“Nothing.” She shrugged. “I guess I’m a little jealous, that’s all.”

“Because you always wanted to be an international racing sensation?” Mark teased from behind her.

“Not exactly,” she chuckled. “More like I’ve always wished for the freedom to go where I wanted when I wanted, to see the world and do what I love.”

“You’re on your way now, right?” Bastian scooped her from

the molded bucket chair onto his lap.

"Yeah, I guess I am." She snuggled against his chest as she recounted all the changes she'd made in the past months then wondered why the thought of striking out on her own didn't thrill her quite as much right then.

"You're going to do great, gorgeous." His hands glided across her back, rubbing the tension from her. The combination of the wine flowing through her and his gentle care had her relaxed in no time. She didn't even flinch when the flight attendant came to clear their dishes.

"Is there anything else I can get for you?"

"We're good, thanks." Sebastian's chest rumbled beneath her cheek with his dismissal. "We won't be needing service until breakfast. Say, an hour before we land?"

"Enjoy the rest of the flight then."

"Oh, we will." Mark uttered the remark under his breath. For their ears only.

Desire flared in her gut. Would they really give her what she yearned for most—the room to stretch her wings and explore without judgment or recrimination?

Yes, they would. The certainty blossomed in her.

Anxious to repay their generosity, she peeked up from her perch. "No more games, no messing around. I want you."

She trailed her fingers over Sebastian's cheek then turned to include Mark. "And you. Right now."

"Who am I to keep a lady waiting?" The navigator rose from his chair across the table then whipped his shirt over his head. The flex of his ridiculous muscles entranced her until he popped the button on his jeans.

Lynn hopped off Sebastian then grasped the hem of his cotton shirt. She tugged it up then over his raised arms. She stood there a moment, memorizing every curve and the play of the soft light on his tan skin.

"What will you do with us, *tesoro*?" Calm, collected and ready for anything, he challenged her to shock him with that curious stare.

Instead of answering, she swayed from side to side as she peeled her blouse from her shoulders then shimmied out of her skirt. Lynn rolled the stockings down her legs, loving the hunger in Sebastian's gaze.

A hiss escaped from between his clenched teeth.

The sound had her smiling when she turned to slip her underwear off, granting him a clear view of her naked ass and back. In the distance, she heard Mark rummaging through the duffle he'd stowed behind their take-off seats.

"Stand up, Bastian." When he did as she commanded, she knelt before him. She'd never had such an overpowering urge to give someone pleasure as she did right now, with this man. After all, he'd taken care of her earlier while seeking nothing in return. She had no doubt he'd do it again now if she were selfish enough to let him.

His hands toyed with the strands of her hair but didn't grab hold, didn't force her in any direction. He waited, with supreme patience, while she counted to ten to keep from begging him to fuck her on the floor. Two minutes of ecstasy wouldn't satisfy her this time.

She eased snug denim from his trim hips, staring as his half-hard cock bobbed along his thigh. Her hands rose, bracing her weight above his knees. Then she dipped her head to take him into her mouth.

"*Dio!* Yes." Light draws of her lips on his lengthening shaft had his breath rushing out in great gasps. She smiled around him as she watched his reaction from beneath her lashes. Working him gently, she eased his length to the back of her mouth, relishing every taste. While she encompassed him with wet heat, she reached out her tongue to lick the raised seam of his sac.

"Damn, sweetheart." Mark's palms landed on her shoulders when he zoomed in for a closer look at her handiwork. "I bet that feels fucking great."

"Does." Sebastian's groan sent a thrill along her spine. She'd learned a thing or two in her sexual encounters she would bet the young hussies they'd been with hadn't bothered to pay attention to yet. Not every man wanted a woman to eat him alive.

Her palms glided up his ripped legs to squeeze his ass. Then she nudged him toward the table. When he caught on, he turned as she came to her feet, keeping his cock buried to the hilt as he reclined. It slid against her tongue. She moaned, causing him to jerk harder in a vicious cycle of arousal.

Bent at the waist, she remained in the perfect position to continue laving him. Sebastian sprawled on his back on the table with his gorgeous ass resting on the edge. She settled between his splayed thighs. He propped each foot on the seat of a chair on either side of her to provide her with easy access. She spread her legs then arched her spine to present herself to Mark.

"You want me to fuck you, *cara*?"

She moaned around Sebastian's shaft, now rock-hard and heavy between her lips.

"Good thing I grabbed these." The crinkle of a wrapper tearing couldn't distract her from her mission.

Lynn relaxed her throat, easing Sebastian farther in until her lips rested on the trunk of his body.

"So good." His hands latched on to the edge of the table beside his tense thighs, allowing her to take her time in torturing him. "You're killing me."

She giggled around him. But not for long.

"Help me out, Mark." His strained plea shot straight to her pussy then up to her heavy breasts, dangling beneath her. "Distract her. I don't want to come like this. Not yet."

He might not want to crash into orgasm, but she sure as hell did. Two young studs would be able to keep up with her all night long if she wished. She didn't have to stifle her reaction as she sometimes did with men her own age.

The head of Mark's cock nudged her slippery vulva, seeking entrance. Each glancing press of his latex-encased shaft had her rocking back to greet it. He teased her, rimming the mouth of her pussy with the blunt head until she thought she might scream in frustration.

Then he notched the tip against her. She clamped down, kissing it with her steamy flesh.

He groaned, blanketing her spine as he reached for her shoulders. When he had her pinned where he liked, he lunged, impaling her on his beefy erection in one fluid thrust.

Stars exploded in her vision. Her eyes flew open, locked with Sebastian's, letting him witness her overwhelming pleasure. A rush of adrenaline left her soaring as one man fucked her while the other watched. She'd expected the experience to be phenomenal, but nothing could have prepared her for this high.

"Yes, gorgeous." Sebastian groaned. "Surrender to it. Let him take you all the way."

Mark's arms came around her—one below her breasts and the other above her hips—when her legs trembled, threatening to collapse. The fingers of his lower hand splayed over her mound, teasing her clit.

A miniature shockwave emanated from the site of his impact. Instincts had her lips curling over her teeth to protect Bastian from her desire. She sucked him harder, her tongue swirling over the ridge on the underside of his cock. Nothing could compare to his pre-cum busting over her taste buds while his friend tunneled deep and slow but steady inside her.

"*Tesoro,* stop." He panted. "Give me a minute."

She shook her head in disagreement, his hard-on slapping the inside of each of her cheeks in the process. Another spurt of his musk splattered on the roof of her mouth.

Mark ground into her harder when he realized what she intended. "Oh yeah. Make him come for you. Swallow him. He won't be able to resist."

Lynn gave Bastian one last lick then glided to the root. His bulging head opened her throat and she gulped around him. Thank God she didn't have a gag reflex.

Mark increased the pace of his fucking, pairing each stroke with a tap from his finger. Her entire body gathered, suffocating his implanted cock.

When Sebastian's heels drummed on the plastic chairs, his head thrashed from side to side. Then his glorious body arched off the table, accompanied by a shout. His contracted balls bobbed against her lips as they pumped his semen down her throat. The elation at conquering his resistance pulled her with him into the maelstrom of passion and surrender.

She came so hard on Mark's cock, she didn't know how the other man kept moving within her. For each pulse of her muscles, she swallowed another draught of Sebastian's seed. After what could have been seconds, or minutes, she purred around his semi-erect flesh.

"You two alive over there?" Mark continued to tunnel inside her throbbing channel.

"Mmm."

Bastian shivered when she moaned, his cock twitching in her loose hold. He levered onto his elbow for a better view then petted her hair as he caught his breath. "That…was the *best* blowjob I've ever had. *Dio,* how can I want more?"

Lynn smirked when his penis began to inflate beneath the gentle laps of her tongue. She let him slide from her mouth for a moment, nuzzling his balls instead.

"That's so hot, *cara.*" Mark withdrew his cock then used it to tap her clit until the ultrasensitivity transformed into renewed desire. Once it had, she ground herself on him again. Satisfied, he slid home, screwing her with short, fast jabs that stoked the embers of her climax. "You're not afraid to take what you want."

"Be gentler with her, Mark." Sebastian would have squirmed away from her if she hadn't increased the suction on his testicle.

"No." Her garbled response was clear enough. "Harder."

"You're sure?" Mark stalled, waiting for confirmation both from her and his best friend.

"Now!"

"Sorry, gorgeous. You're the boss." Sebastian grimaced then nodded at the other man. "Give her what she wants."

"You better get back in the game. Need to tag you soon. Not gonna last." In fact, Mark's breathing had already become erratic and his hands moved to grope her breasts. The pressure on her hard nipples felt divine.

"You love driving us wild, don't you?" Bastian traced her mouth around the edge of his balls.

"Mmm." She gasped as Mark's blunt dick hit a sweet spot.

"Right there, *amico.*"

The guys' coordinated efforts had her entire body compressing again. She'd never been so turned-on in all her life. Their expert lovemaking blew her mind. Mark bent lower then bit her shoulder. His abs slapped her ass faster and faster, but the stud ground his cock against her G-spot each time until she couldn't resist a moment longer.

She abandoned Sebastian's rejuvenated hard-on to scream out her pleasure. Mark slammed inside her one final time then poured his release into the condom he wore, all the while muttering things she couldn't understand but didn't need to.

All that mattered was the fire raging in Sebastian's eyes when she glanced up at him.

"Come here." He tugged her onto the table with him, her knees straddling his trim hips, to claim her mouth. And no matter how his best friend had pleased her, something about kissing this man held more significance. The attraction flowed between them, instant and powerful.

"One more," she whispered against his lips, feeling greedy.

"As many as you like."

"One more," she repeated. "With you."

She let her forehead rest on his while she caught her breath for a minute. When Mark groaned from behind her, she turned to check on him. A wry grin twisted his lush mouth as he hunched with hands on thighs, looking as wobbly as a newborn deer.

"My new favorite dessert." He sank to his knees, sparking a wicked thought.

Lynn rolled in Sebastian's arms, coming to rest with her back nestled to his front. She wiggled until she sat up and could plant one foot on each of his thighs. He caught on quick, this man of hers. Before she could ask, he cupped her hips, supporting her, lifting her as she reached for his erection.

A whimper escaped when his longer, thicker hard-on stretched her engorged tissue. She'd always enjoyed the reverse cowgirl position, but this time somehow surpassed all others.

"Okay?" At least he didn't try to stop her this time.

"Perfect," she sighed when her ass met his abdomen, embedding him in her completely. His hands curled around her sides to wander up her belly to her chest, pinching her nipples then rubbing out the sting. His fingers roamed over her entire body, everywhere he could reach, waking up nerves she thought deadened by her prior orgasms.

Mark absorbed every touch with his rekindled stare from his spot in front of her.

She started fucking Sebastian with slow pumps of her hips, building the pleasure one final time. It might be another two years until she had sex again after this night. Her movements turned urgent when she considered her simple affair had only hours to go before it burned out. She would take what the men offered—drown herself in ecstasy so she never forgot what it had been like to shine in their arms.

She performed for Mark. He definitely got off on watching. From a foot away, he could see the minute details of her and Sebastian's joining. The flex of her pussy around her lover's cock, the flush of their skin as blood raced to their loins, the gradual scrunching of his best friend's scrotum as she picked up steam.

"Lick my clit, Mark." The man drifted closer to where she and Sebastian were joined at the edge of the table but stopped, in the double vee of their thighs, an inch short of her pussy and his best friend's cock. The heat of his breath washing over her as his chest bellowed drove her to beg, "Please."

He groaned then closed the gap, enfolding her tight bundle of nerves between his lips. After their intense fucking, she appreciated his gentle manipulation. Her eyes rolled in her skull when Sebastian countered with long, liquid glides of his hips that filled her with his cock.

Suddenly, the tender loving took her higher than all the rough fucking in the world. Between the fluttering swipes of Mark's tongue and the easy pressure of Sebastian's erection, she curled her toes in delight on Bastian's knees.

"Mark." She whimpered as she tried to hold on. She wasn't finished yet. Not without Sebastian and he needed something more than this delicate sway to get off.

The man between her legs angled his head until their gazes met and his attention focused on her.

"Put one of your fingers in his ass."

Sebastian went stiff beneath her. "What? I'm not gay, Lynn. Not bi either."

She lifted off him until the bare tip of his cock remained embedded then sank onto him bit by bit. "I'm not asking you to let him fuck you. You said I could have anything I wanted. You'll like this. Trust me as I've trusted you."

The urge to lead him somewhere he'd never gone before raged inside her. It was only fair after what he'd done to her—destroyed her for other men.

His hands tightened on her hips until she guaranteed she'd have bruises to show for it but the pressure ratcheted her arousal higher. He didn't object further. Mark stared at her in wonder but no hint of disgust dimmed the appetite she saw in his chocolate eyes.

"Go ahead, you know you want to," she dared him.

All three of them groaned together when Mark's finger slid beside the length of Sebastian's cock inside her, gathering her wetness. Then he retreated. The sight of his long finger poised to penetrate Sebastian had the beginnings of another orgasm looming near.

"Seb?" He hesitated.

"Fuck." The cock buried in her pussy swelled to epic proportions a second before her lover groaned, "Do it."

More of her lubrication trickled around Sebastian, onto his balls. She observed Mark's thick digit disappearing beneath them.

An extensive string of Italian poured from the man she rode as his best friend plundered his virgin ass. She laughed out loud when his cock bulged inside her. "I told you so."

"Yes!"

"Now finish what you started." She balanced on one hand, planted on Sebastian's chest behind her, and reached for Mark's hair with the other, but he came forward on his own. He turned sideways to make room for his mouth to latch on to her pussy while he continued to ream Sebastian in counterpoint to her escalating thrusts.

She ground against them both—Mark on each forward motion and Sebastian on the reverse. Her torso slithered like a snake as she maximized the contact with the pleasure-inducing bookends.

Her head tipped back, inviting Sebastian to strain upward to kiss her. Their tongues tangled. She stared into his eyes, hoping he could detect even a fraction of the joy he had gifted her. He smiled near her mouth then nipped her lip as he picked up the pace.

A tsunami of passion barreled down on her, so tall and strong she feared it might annihilate her. She tried to escape, but running from Mark's mouth impaled her on Sebastian, and going the other way wasn't any better. She couldn't avoid the impending destruction.

Lynn gasped, prepared to warn the men servicing her.

"What the..." Sebastian froze beneath her for a heartbeat then hammered her. The hitch in his stride shoved her closer to Mark's talented mouth, which now vibrated with his ragged moans. "He's coming. On my leg."

The idea of Mark's hot ejaculate splashing over Sebastian's furred shin sent her into orbit. Sebastian couldn't remain unaffected in the wake of their orgasms. His cock plumped inside her, the ridges of his veins amplifying the best climax of her life until she thought she might pass out.

She screamed, "Bastian!"

His arms banded around her, sheltering her while every muscle in her body seized and jerked. She crashed through dozens of spasms. The answering shouts, groans and grunts of the two men echoed around her until, at last, they melted into a tangle of arms, legs and shattered inhibitions.

They didn't stay that way long. She needed to see Sebastian instead of staring at the curved ceiling. Neither the table nor the floor ranked high on the most comfortable places to lie either.

Sebastian sat up, helping her to her feet. She whimpered when his soft cock slipped from her juicy pussy. Instead of slinking away from Mark, he extended his hand to help his friend up then grinned.

Thank God.

"Next time your chin comes anywhere near my balls, you're gonna have to shave first. Like fucking sandpaper, dude." Both Lynn and Mark laughed when Sebastian winced then rearranged his package.

"Didn't hear you complaining when her pussy practically squeezed your dick in half. Besides, it serves you right for cheating in our game, you bastard."

She stared at Mark, her jaw hanging open. "You knew? Then why…?"

"It's what I wanted too." He placed a sweet kiss on the corner of her mouth. "You were amazing tonight. The best."

Sebastian shuddered then took her hand. "Let's go. Shower time."

"Thank you," she whispered over her shoulder as Bastian led her toward the private cabin.

* * * * *

Soaking in a garden tub on a jet speeding through the sky didn't seem as odd as allowing Sebastian—a man she'd just met, a younger man, a man she cared too much about—to tend to the aches dotting her body. Still, she enjoyed the intimacy of the act. She'd watched him rinse his best friend's cum from his calf before drawing the steamy water for them to soak in.

Now she lounged between his legs, nestled against his slick chest as he dragged a soapy cloth over her torso. When his hand plunged below the water to wash her pussy, he swallowed so hard she heard it.

"It's okay, Bastian," she whispered. "I'm clean. And I've been on the Pill since I was twenty. I don't know if I could even have children anymore."

"I've never forgotten to wear a condom before."

She turned to face him. His heart pounded beneath her palm. "I've never failed to insist on it. So I guess we're even."

"Do you think I'm a poor excuse for a man because I don't want children? I hear other guys talk about passing on their legacy…" He shrugged.

The serious concern in his tone coupled with lines of strain she didn't like seeing at the corner of his luscious mouth. "If it does, then I'm in the same boat. Don't get me wrong, I like kids. But I can't see myself having them. I guess that's one of the reasons I never got married."

"I'm not stable enough. I travel all the time. No kid should have to have an absentee parent or be dragged across creation, away from all their friends. I don't see myself wanting to leave what I do. I love racing. Even when I can't drive anymore, I want to be a chief. Or maybe an owner someday."

"I respect you for knowing what you want, refusing to compromise and taking responsibility to ensure you don't impact anyone else. You're a good man, Sebastian. Never doubt that."

The kiss he shared with her overflowed with gratitude and relief.

Disaster averted, they soaked together while talking about nothing important in hushed whispers until the water had gone cold and their skin wrinkled.

Lynn yawned as he carried her to the thick mattress then deposited her on a pile of pillows covered in bedding as fluffy as a cloud. She burrowed into them then held out her arms, welcoming him beside her.

"I can't tell you how many times I'd have traded a year's worth of Belgian chocolate for a bed while trying to sleep sitting up on a flight across the Atlantic. Now I'd give anything to stay awake a little while longer." She fought the tears stinging her eyes. If she closed her lids, she knew she wouldn't be able to open them again. And, all too soon, they'd be going their separate ways.

"Isn't that the truth." Sebastian tucked her close then sighed. "We'll dream together, *tesoro*."

"Promise?"

"I do."

"Goodnight, Bastian."

"'Night, gorgeous."

Chapter Seven

Lynn woke to unfiltered sunlight glinting from the cracks in the fancy shades covering the porthole-style windows. She rolled over, searching for Bastian with one hand. She found the warm depression where he'd rested but no man shared her bed.

So that was that.

She swung her legs over the side of the mattress, dragging the sheet with her like a toga. If he couldn't stand to wake up with her, she didn't want to flash her middle-aged imperfections in the harsh light of day for him to scrutinize.

Come on, what did you expect after a one-night stand? Just because she'd never done it before didn't mean she had no idea of the way people played the game.

A glance at her watch confirmed they had less than thirty minutes until they landed. He hadn't woken her for breakfast. Less awkward conversation that way, she supposed. She wrangled the spare set of clothes she'd stashed in her carry-on from the bag then consulted the bathroom mirror. It'd been a long while since she looked this alive. She'd take that.

Still, she had to plaster a fake smile across her face when she slipped into the main cabin. Mark occupied the same chair he had during takeoff, flipping through a motorsport magazine. Sebastian had gone missing.

"Good morning, *cara.* I was about to wake you. We need to strap in for landing."

"And Sebastian…" She hated that she'd asked but she had to know.

"Uh…he's taking care of some business in the crew quarters."

"I see." She dropped into the seat opposite him then feigned interest in the clouds coming closer with the passing miles. Not even the gorgeous formations could interest her this morning.

"Breakfast is on the table if you'd like a bagel, some eggs…yogurt?"

"I'm not hungry, thanks."

"At least let me get you some coffee—"

"Mark, stop." She winced at the bitterness in her command then whispered, "Please."

Lynn couldn't stand for the man to feel obligated to clean up his partner's mess. She had to keep it together long enough to make the world's longest walk of shame through the jet bridge and out of the airport.

"I'm here if you need anything, *cara*."

"Thank you."

And with that, he left her in peace for the remainder of the flight.

* * * * *

After landing, Mark helped her with her luggage then kept her company as they disembarked. What kind of fool did it make her that she still hoped Sebastian would show at the last moment? He'd checked every box on her wish list and then some in their oh-so-brief Cougar affair. She hoped they could part on favorable terms to keep the memories bright, untarnished.

Mark turned to her as they neared the exit to the cab lanes. People streamed by in all directions across Paris' congested airport. She planned to take the metro to her favorite hotel in the Etoile district, so she slowed to say goodbye when he peeled off.

"Are you going to recommend private jets in your guides?"

"Best in-flight service, hands down."

Mark threw back his head as he laughed. "Thank you, *cara*. For me too."

Lynn attempted a smile then angled her head so he wouldn't

notice her sniffle.

"Ah, damn." He wrapped an arm around her shoulders. "I have no idea what *il bastardo* is thinking this morning…"

"Don't make excuses. He doesn't owe me anything." She accepted Mark's comforting hug. A few more seconds then she'd buck up and start off on her own.

"He's never pulled something like this before. You really got to him. Still, this is no way to treat a lady. I swear I'll kick his ass for you, okay?"

"How about a knee to the balls?"

"Deal." He kissed her cheek. "I don't suppose there's any chance you'd call *me* if I gave you my number, is there?"

Why couldn't exhilaration make her heart dance at the idea of a relationship with Mark the way it had for Sebastian? Sure, they'd had steaming-hot sex, but she'd conned herself into believing there'd been a spark, something greater than the physical, between her and the young driver.

"Oh *affunculo* no." Sebastian stepped between her and Mark, knocking the card from the navigator's fingers in the process.

"Look who decided to show up," Mark snarled, prepared to battle for her, but Sebastian ignored him.

"Shit. I'm sorry, *tesoro*." The endearment caused her to cringe. How could he mean it now? Had the whole thing been an act? "I was on the phone. Didn't realize they'd opened the doors. Thank God I caught you. We need to talk."

Lynn would rather wait in the absurd line outside the Louvre with all the suckers who didn't purchase advance tickets online on a Wednesday morning in July than listen to what Bastian had to say at that moment. Why couldn't he let her go with her dignity intact?

She'd already planned to stop by her favorite patisserie for a decadent fruit tart then wallow in her hotel for a few hours before burying the disappointment and savoring the wicked aches he'd inspired. But he refused to let her brush him off.

"Grab a taxi, Mark? I'll be out in a minute."

The other man looked to her for confirmation before nodding. "Safe travels, *cara*."

He left with a wave.

Sebastian meshed their fingers together as though nothing

odd had happened. "I have to head out. We're taking the TGV to Toulouse. But I have a surprise for you."

"You do?" *Why?* She racked her brain for some parting gift to give him in return. Like maybe her middle finger jammed into his gut.

"Yeah. I called my mom this morning and arranged for you to stay with her when you get to Erchie. It took some juggling to shift your reservation from Caprietto's but we worked it out. I can't wait for her to meet you. Then I figured you could swing by the circuit when we pass through Rome. I didn't plan for it to take so long but it's a bitch scheduling stuff this time of year. Tourists everywhere. But…all the tickets are here." He shoved an envelope at her. "You can write a whole book about Rome, right?"

She stared at him for a solid five seconds, trying to convince herself he was joking.

"You did *what*?" She scrubbed her hand over her cheeks. This couldn't be happening. "You didn't even stay this morning and now you're telling me you intended for there to be more?"

"Wait, you thought I was making a clean break?" He cursed under his breath in Italian. "It killed me to leave you sleeping like an angel when all I wanted was to hold you. Or maybe slip in some morning loving. But I thought it more important to make sure we see each other again than to get my rocks off in another meaningless encounter."

"Last night was *meaningless* to you?" She sucked in a breath through her shattered chest. "Great. Maybe we better go our separate ways before this gets any worse. It's been…fun, Sebastian."

She spun, but his hand gripped her shoulder.

"No. Shit, Lynn, this is all coming out wrong."

"Why didn't you talk to me? Why didn't you let us decide together how things would go?" His manipulation betrayed her. "You know how I feel. I thought you understood how important it is for me to be independent…to decide my own fate."

"I do. But… There wasn't time. I didn't think. Don't you know how many girls have asked me for this privilege? I've never invited a woman to tour with me."

She recoiled as though he'd slapped her. "I'm supposed to be grateful for your interference? You arrogant—"

Mark leaned in the sliding door with an apologetic shrug before she could really pour on the steam. "Seb, we have to get a move on or we'll miss the train."

"One minute!"

The frustration radiating from him erased some of yesterday's bliss. She couldn't bear to have him obscure all the glory of the night before with this disastrous parting. "I can't do this, Sebastian. Please. Go. Good luck."

She reached up to kiss his cheek, frozen in shock, then gathered her luggage before spinning on her heel and darting between a baggage trolley and a tour group. By the time she'd crossed the busy lobby and turned, Sebastian had vanished.

* * * * *

LynnLuvs2Trvl: Younger men suck. Immature, cocky, bullheaded…

Rachel: You're starting to sound like my crotchety Aunt Imelda.

LynnLuvs2Trvl: Oh God. I am, aren't I? But it's been two weeks! Why the hell can't I forget about him?

Rachel: Maybe because he's emailed you every day, desperate for another chance?

LynnLuvs2Trvl: Thanks for giving him my address, by the way. I never would have thought you'd do that!

Rachel: He begged on the blog. He sounded so sincere. Despite what you think right now, there's something here, Lynn. I think you should answer him.

LynnLuvs2Trvl: I'd have to read his messages to answer them. I've deleted every one without opening it. For all we know, he's making sure he didn't knock me up.

Rachel: Lynn! You didn't!

LynnLuvs2Trvl: I did. I refuse to be tied to anyone. Especially not a controlling, infantile— Argh! You get the point. But now I'm screwed. I'm not with him and I can't stop thinking about him. I even went to the Rally Racing Museum today, like that's a top-five destination for a solo woman's travel guide. His picture was freaking everywhere. Do you have any idea how cute a man in a jumpsuit is?

Rachel: Holy crap, Lynn. This is getting out of hand. If you miss him this much, why not call him? Email, whatever.

LynnLuvs2Trvl: After what happened? No way. I can't stay with a man who wants to control me.

Rachel: If he's still dogging you, he's probably open to discussing your boundaries. You barely know each other. The way I figure, it'd have been easy for you both to write the night off but neither of you have.

LynnLuvs2Trvl: Worse, I leave for Erchie tonight. I tried everything. Including a bribe. But I couldn't get my original hotel back. There's no way he told his mom about us, right?

Rachel: That he fucked you in a limo an hour after meeting you then shared you with his best friend for a wild night that I am super envious of? Probably not. But I'm betting he raved about the gorgeous woman he met. You know, enough to make it uncomfortable.

LynnLuvs2Trvl: Damn it. That's what I thought too.

Rachel: Sorry, Lynn.

Lynn paused before exiting the deserted station to stretch her knotted muscles with a whimper. Nothing like hours on the regional train interspersed with mad dashes through terminals—traversing flights of stairs to platforms that never seemed close together with even the lightest luggage when attempting a quick connection—to tire a girl out.

On top of that, she'd gotten burned by notes she'd found online that cited the town's reliable tram system but had failed to mention it wouldn't be completed for another five years at least. If the dusty donation jar she'd spotted gave any indication, Erchie might never go high-tech. And that was part of its appeal.

She probably could have caught a straggling cab if she hadn't stopped to use the restroom. By the time she brushed her hair and popped a mint, in case Mrs. Fiori sized her up, the skeleton crew had departed. No one remained to listen to the buzz of the florescent lights but her.

These were exactly the hints she could capitalize on for her book. Though it didn't do *her* much good. She had a hard time imagining anything sinister lurking in the peaceful town when the *swoosh* of the ocean sang in the background. Still, survival instincts she'd honed over years of traveling alone had her dreading the walk through twilit streets to her accommodations.

Grabbing the last train into town had been a mistake.

Thank God she could cross the distance to the bed and breakfast in fifteen minutes at a brisk pace. She hauled her bag along the ramp, surprised to see a car running with its lights on at the curb.

Lynn had taken two giant strides along the sidewalk when the car inched forward. The window began to roll down. *Great.*

She picked up her pace, the wheels of her suitcase squeaking in protest.

"*Buona sera, signorina.*"

Lynn debated ignoring the older gentleman but opted for a tiny wave as she continued along her way. Still, he persisted, the Peugeot creeping along to stay even with her.

"*Scusami.*" The white-haired man flailed his hands in her peripheral vision.

Then he said two magical words. The only two that could have claimed her attention. "Sebastian Fiori."

She tripped over a crack in the sidewalk. At least she tried to convince herself something other than the instant rush of anticipation and longing caused her stumble.

Her stare whipped in the man's direction. Now that she really looked, she found countless similarities to the perfection she had memorized two weeks ago. The sappy part of her had feared she'd forget his face after such a short time together but the opposite had been true. Every night, visions of him had filled her imagination.

Almost as though they still dreamed together.

When she shook her head to clear the ridiculous thoughts, the man's eyebrow arched.

"Mrs. Fiori…hotel…ride…"

The man struggled with English but she understood. Sebastian came by his tendency to grab the reins naturally it seemed. She bit her lip as she considered accepting. To be honest, refusing the kind gesture would make her stupid *and* rude in this case.

She smiled. "*Grazie.*"

Before she could lug her bag to the vehicle, the man had hopped out. He shooed her away while he took care of hoisting it into the hatchback. Then he turned to her, planting a double-cheeked air kiss on her. When they parted, he slapped his chest. "*Eduardo. Zio.*"

Ah, Sebastian's uncle. No wonder.

"Lynn."

The man nodded. Since they couldn't converse, Eduardo cranked up the zesty Italian folk music bouncing through the car's tinny speakers. She laughed in delight when he belted out the harmonies, encouraging her to clap along. His charisma was impossible to resist. Another trait that ran in the family, she supposed.

Just as Eduardo delivered the rousing finale, they swung into a narrow stone driveway.

The charming terracotta-tile-roofed villa nestled in a field of wild flowers and citrus trees. Perched on a low outcropping, it overlooked the warm waters of the Mediterranean, cerulean even at dusk. The hue of the waves washing the shore reminded her of Sebastian's eyes.

But before regret could overwhelm her, Eduardo cupped her elbow. He guided her toward the rear of the structure with a knowing smile. The crowd of laughing, drinking, joking locals gathered around an outdoor fire pit and a TV—plugged in via an enormous extension cord from the main house—surprised her.

Bright red and blue pennants adorned with Driven Wild and Sebastian's team logo strung across the lush yard, creating a ceiling over the gathered tables piled with pastries and wine. Eduardo whisked her suitcase inside before she could stop him. When she followed, a woman carrying a checked hand towel greeted her with a smile.

"You are Lynn Madison?"

"Mrs. Fiori?"

"*Si,* Maria." The woman welcomed her with open arms. In two seconds flat, she'd been smothered in a giant squeezy hug against Sebastian's mother's ample cleavage without so much as a hint of the appraising stare she'd dreaded. "Welcome to Erchie and to our home. You are just in time!"

"Thank you. Truly." Lynn tried to focus on Mrs. Fiori's easy acceptance despite the whispers spreading through the gathering like wildfire. More than one young woman shot her a glare sharp enough to sting across the patio. "Am I interrupting? I can go for a walk until your event is finished. Unless there's something I help with?"

"Not at all! You'll sit. Watch the race? Sebastian starts in five minutes." A hint of unease crept into the gracious host's eyes, which reminded her so much of the man who'd rocked her world.

"Tonight? I didn't realize..." God, flying along ridiculous courses in the dark! Why hadn't she considered the dangers inherent in his job? She reached out without thinking to pat Maria's hand where it wrung her apron. "I would like that very much."

They sank to a rustic bench together. Someone thrust a glass into her hand, the maroon wine sloshing onto her fingers as they passed by. What must it be like to have so many people rooting for you, supporting you? Sebastian had innumerable ties here yet still he seemed free to do as he pleased.

Could there be a difference between a bond and a restraint?

She took a slug of the cheap wine, savoring the burn as it slid through her system. The commentators finished their run-through of tonight's stage, the final section of this event. Lynn cringed when she studied the insane wiggles in the gravel course. Unease skittered along her spine, inciting a shiver.

"These are the worst for me to watch." Maria polished off her own drink then snagged a replacement. "He's leading by almost two minutes. He could play safe. But my son does not know how."

In the background, a flashy graphic plotted Sebastian's current time versus the world record. At this point, he edged out in front by several seconds. Never mind that he held the top five ranks, she knew he'd do his best to shatter his previous mark.

"How long will it last?" Her ignorance rankled. Why hadn't she paid closer attention to the facts at the museum instead of staring at his tight ass in all the pictures?

“This stage…twenty-seven kilometers.” Maria nodded as she considered, “I bet he will finish in no more than ten minutes.”

Some quick mental math had her eyebrows rising. “In these conditions?”

Maria didn’t answer. Instead she made the sign of the cross then focused in on the television. People stood and cheered as three electronic beeps heralded the launch. Then, in a cloud of dust, Sebastian’s car rocketed from the starting line. She could see two shadows inside the cabin of the car but couldn’t make out either Sebastian or Mark’s features behind the thick helmets they wore.

The cheers of the Fiori’s friends, neighbors and relatives brought the night alive. Lynn couldn’t believe how fast the bright car flew through twists and turns. The slides over treacherous lines left razor-thin margins of error. Each time Sebastian nailed a section, the gathering grew more rowdy until catcalls, whistles and yells drowned out the sound from the television not two feet in front of her.

Lynn took her focus from the screen for a millisecond to observe the outpouring of pure excitement for a man who had obviously touched many people in his lifetime. She didn’t need to see the screen to know something had gone horribly wrong when the crowd hushed mid-cheer. A glass shattered in the background as it hit the pavers.

Her head whipped around to see Sebastian’s car crash through the underbrush and clip the corner of a stone wall. It jolted to a stop, nose down in a ditch. The pain in her chest as her heart skipped a few beats alarmed her in the far recesses of her mind. She couldn’t say who’d moved first but Maria clenched her hand so tight she thought her knuckles might crack, and Lynn returned the favor.

Though it seemed an eternity of uncertain terror passed, seconds later, a communal sigh of relief washed over her when the lights on Sebastian’s car flicked three times in rapid succession.

“His sign to me.” Maria explained between whispered prayers of thanks.

Lynn watched, numb, as Mark and Sebastian erupted from the vehicle then pushed it out of the rut, onto the course. Her eyes nearly bugged out of her skull when the crazy bastards piled into the deathtrap and took off along the route.

As though the world hadn't ground to a stop, cheers blanketed her again. But nothing could chase the chill from her bones. Both because she feared for Sebastian's safety in the remainder of the race and because she could no longer deny how deep he'd embedded himself in her heart during their *meaningless* night together.

She stayed long enough to watch him clamber onto the roof of his dented vehicle with Mark. The roar of the hometown crowd—not to mention the shower of champagne dousing them—making it clear they'd won yet another race.

Then she staggered to her feet. Maria rose with her, throwing an arm around Lynn's waist. She understood Lynn's sudden desire for solitude, guiding her through the cheerful citrus colored décor to Sebastian's room.

"I wish I could say the wrecks get easier but I can't." When Lynn didn't answer Maria's soothing rambling, the woman continued. "You've had a long day. I think some sleep would do you well."

The older woman flipped on the bare overhead light, casting the cozy space in a warm glow. Every inch of plaster had been covered by framed articles on her son's success. One corner held a rustic bookshelf buried in trophies. The bed had been turned down with fresh sheets, flowers spread over the pillow.

The idea of sleeping here, surrounded by the man she would never forget—but had already lost—had her aching and on edge. "Why are you doing this? Why let me stay here? I am nothing to him. To you."

"I've always wished one thing for my son. They say I spoil him but I want him to have everything he desires, no matter how big the dream. Sebastian says you're special to him."

"How can he know? We're almost strangers. And I'm so much older than him! Doesn't that bother you?"

"Hearts know nothing of time—not age or length of acquaintance. They know only what they need. The moment I met my husband, I knew. Here." Maria collected Lynn's hand, clasped it in her own as she touched it to the place over her heart. "My son has never said this to me before, please understand.

You two are destined."

Lynn concentrated on preventing her eyes from rolling. A couple of wild fucks between strangers couldn't be written off as cosmic intervention. More like irrational, reckless and decadent decision making.

"You do not believe."

"In fate? No, I'm sorry."

"Then think of how you miss him. Call it whatever you like. I can see the truth in your eyes. Your fear for him is as deep as mine. I believe you are special and I would not have you hurt. That would cause my son pain."

Maria hugged her then turned to go. "Sleep well, Lynn. Sebastian says he dreams with you still."

Lynn sagged onto the comforting flannel sheets. She sighed as she burrowed into Sebastian's bed, deluding herself into thinking she caught the scent of him on the pillow.

That must have been why visions of him surrounded her all night long.

Chapter Eight

Lynn tipped her chin to catch rays of the mid-afternoon sun on her face. With her eyes closed, she savored the breeze fluffing her hair, making her gauzy sarong dance around her legs. She curled her toes in the damp sand, at peace for the first time in many months.

She'd decided.

Today she would read Sebastian's emails—she hadn't yet emptied her recycle bin—with an open mind before sending him a note in return. Maybe she'd get his number from Maria so she could hear his voice again. Just for a minute.

She could admit to herself that she'd overreacted now. Yes, he'd gone too far but she'd worried so much about her precious freedom that she'd overlooked the difference between a leash and an invitation.

Regret had her sighing as she considered the time she'd wasted. Unwilling to exacerbate her mistake, she pivoted, heading for the netbook she'd stowed in her room. Sebastian's room.

Her foot froze mid-step when she caught sight of the man ambling toward her.

He hesitated, as though unsure of his welcome, but she couldn't deny the thrill that raced through her at the sight of him. His unbuttoned shirt rippled in the gentle wind, revealing the perfection of his sculpted torso above low-slung cargo shorts.

Olive skin shone, making her fingers tingle with the need to explore.

But his piercing blue eyes, shadowed with uncertainty, had her bolting across the distance between them until she molded to his solid chest.

He wrapped her in a bear hug then whispered in her hair, "*Come, mi sei mancata!*"

"Did you just call me pasta?" She separated the scant inch necessary to peek up at him.

"Definitely not," he laughed. "Though you look good enough to eat. *Dio*, I missed you."

"Same here," she sighed. Before she could think better of it, her fingertips traced the gash on his bold cheekbone. "You scared me half to death last night."

"Sorry 'bout that, *tesoro*." His head dipped, his lips nearing hers. "But I'm glad to hear you still care. I thought I might have ruined everything. Ruined this…"

Lynn's breath caught in her lungs when Sebastian kissed her. Their lips brushed then melded as they both took and received in turn. The sparks she'd thought she'd amplified in her memory flared between them, setting her on fire.

Sebastian scooped her into his arms, her ass resting in his broad palms as she wrapped her legs around his trim waist. She practically climbed him in her desperation to get closer. He walked them to the water's edge, slipping behind an outcropping of rock, shielding them from anyone who might be watching from inside.

He laid her in the soft sand, following her down. "Lynn, wait—"

"Talk later." She yanked the hem of his shirt over his head, stripping the well-worn fabric off his shoulders. "Please, Bastian, show me you still feel it too. Nothing else matters."

For long minutes they lost themselves in the simple pleasure of kissing—tasting, nipping and licking—until the bliss overwhelmed reason. She had to have him again, had to fuse them until separation became impossible.

"Wait, *tesoro*." Sebastian groaned as he lifted off her. "I need you to know this is not meaningless to me. Far from it."

"Shh." Lynn gathered him close once more, peppering his

face, neck and shoulders with kisses. "Not for me either."

"Thank God." Waves lapped at their toes where their legs tangled on the beach. He bracketed her face with gentle hands then sipped from her lips as he nudged her thighs apart to make room for his frame in the cradle of her hips.

His hard cock branded her through the khaki shorts separating their heat. She plunged her hands beneath the waistband then grabbed his bare ass under the fabric.

"Ever make love on the beach before, Bastian?"

"I've never had sex like this. Not in the daylight, out of the water, where anyone could see if they walk by or pass in a boat." He tossed a glance over his shoulder to be sure no one lurked in the background. His sudden modesty amused her, tempting her to push him until he murmured, "And I've never made love to a woman in my life. But I'd like to try it with you."

"Same here." She rolled, tucking him beneath her as she straddled his hips. While he licked his lips, she reached behind her to loosen the tie on her bikini top.

Bastian's hands glided over the sides and back of her thighs, allowing her to reveal herself to his hungry stare. When she'd tugged the laces free from their bow, she dropped her hands to her waist and allowed the fabric to flutter from her breasts.

"So gorgeous," he growled as he gripped her shoulder then tipped her forward until he could surround the tip of one mound with his lips. He flicked his tongue across the puckered surface of her nipple, causing a moan to escape from her parted mouth.

While he drove her insane with his sensual assault, she loosened the strings at her hips then peeled the scrap of her bathing suit from between her legs. The crotch of the fabric glistened in the sunlight, drenched with her arousal.

"You smell delicious." He shimmied lower, his hands bracing her waist until she hovered over his face. "Come to me. Let me taste you."

Her spine arched—hands bracing behind her on his raised knees—when his talented tongue traced the furrows of her pussy. He sipped the slick honey from her with aching delicateness that had her heart blossoming in her chest.

Tender swipes of his lips on her clit primed her for something deeper, stronger. She squirmed in his hold, dragging the soaked folds of her pussy over his chin when her instincts took control. Her hands fisted in the material of his shorts in a weak attempt at divesting him of the damn things before she came without him.

A frustrated whimper clued him in to her plight. He rolled, tugging her to the sand next to him. In two seconds flat, he'd lifted his hips and slid the shorts off, kicking them to the side. He cuddled her into his arms so they lay on their right sides, her back plastered to his chest.

The thick length of his hard-on pressed between her legs, stroking her soaked slit. Sebastian buried one arm in the sand beneath her then draped the other over her waist, giving him complete access to touch her breasts, her belly and her clit. She tilted her head to the left, meeting his seeking lips for another scorching kiss.

He rocked into her in time to his tongue, thrusting against the palate of her mouth. The plump head of his cock stroked her pussy, nudging her closer and closer to ecstasy.

"I want you inside me." She gasped when he angled his hips, probing a bit deeper on the next pass. "Please, Bastian."

He reached around her hip, using two fingers on the underside of his cock to feed it into her waiting clutches. The initial penetration left her trembling. The sweet pressure of him working inside her drove her mad with desire.

When he wedged in the swollen depths of her channel, he slid his hand from his cock to the inside of her knee. He lifted her leg, spreading her until she feared she might split open from the decadent force of his invasion.

"So tight," he groaned near her ear. "*Molto dolce.*"

The flex and release of his toned abdomen stroked his shaft over her sensitive flesh. Slow, deep and controlled, he massaged her from within. Curls of flame licked her abdomen, making it difficult to breathe without calling out her satisfaction. When the fingers of his spread hand strayed from her belly to circle her clit, she cried his name over and over.

The dual sensations primed her body while his affectionate ministrations had her heart clenching in her chest. As they strained together, his cock flared inside her. The defined ridges of his veins teased her inflamed nerve endings. She panted, trying to smother the urge to shatter. She didn't want their passion to end so soon.

But resistance didn't get her far. The harder she fought, the more he focused. He tapped the bump of her clit in time to his thrusts. She stiffened, her pussy clamping on his shaft. She screamed as she came apart in his arms, trusting him to drive her orgasm.

Through the hurricane of desire, he maintained his pace, gritting his teeth above her. When she could process thought beyond the overwhelming ecstasy drowning her, she sighed. He hadn't come with her. Without his pleasure, hers seemed pale and incomplete.

Lynn rolled to her stomach, offering herself for his use. She wanted nothing more than to provide him the means for satisfaction, for half the joy he'd gifted her. She spread her legs then raised her hips, her face pillowed in the sand.

Sebastian couldn't refuse her offer. He pumped into her from behind, driving her into the warm earth. She absorbed his powerful thrusts. His fingers laced with hers as he pinned one wrist to either side of her head.

All vestiges of his gentleness vanished as he staked his claim. She welcomed him, rocking back to meet his thrusts. His chin landed on her shoulder when he dropped lower, covering her back. Without thinking, she angled her head, exposing her neck. He shouted something in Italian then fit deeper within her.

A sense of power washed over her. She could give this to her man and, in doing so, set them both free. The knowledge fanned the embers of her passion, renewing the spasms of her pussy around him in an endless orgasm.

Bastian attacked the vulnerable skin without hesitation. His teeth sank into the crook of her neck and shoulder as he pummeled her. A roar of primal completion echoed around them as he claimed her. The hot splash of his cum pouring deep inside her followed.

Instead of panic, a sense of rightness descended over Lynn. She allowed herself simply to react to the magic their coupling generated. The rush of her climax peaked as the last of Sebastian's seed jetted inside her womb.

Together they collapsed onto the beach, too exhausted to sort through what had happened. She closed her eyes as she snuggled into his chest, content to drift off for a few minutes before dealing with reality.

When Lynn jostled awake, she found herself cradled in Sebastian's lap in the shade of the rock outcropping. He'd gathered her sarong and used it to cover most of her skin.

"Sorry, *tesoro*." He beamed down at her. "I was afraid you'd burn. You're so…white."

She laughed. "I know. I can't tan at all. I go from pink to red."

"You're gorgeous the way you are."

Their gazes met and held for a solid thirty seconds. Then they both spoke at once. "Where—"

"What—"

Sebastian gestured for her to finish but she shook her head. "No, go ahead. What were you going to say?"

He took a deep breath then nodded before asking, "Where will you be next Monday? My races end on Sunday. I have a two-week hiatus after that."

"Florence, I think. It depends…on how my research goes. I could try—"

He cut her off with a finger on her lips before she could offer a compromise she might come to regret. "Do what you have to do. I'll always find you. Wherever you are is where I want to go…if I'm welcome there."

Tears blurred his perfect, if sand-covered, features. Could it be possible?

"And if someday you decide you want to come with me—see the world and do your research from my circuit stops, I'd be honored."

"Can we take things one step at a time?" If she thought that far ahead, she'd get too scared of losing everything and she'd screw it all up.

"Absolutely. Let me begin the journey with you and it'll all work out, *amore mio*."

"Promise?"

"I do."

"Then we'd better go tell your mother the good news." Lynn tied her bikini before waiting for him to tug on his shorts. His grin lit up his entire face as he scrambled to his feet.

She tore up the beach toward the sanctuary of his house, Sebastian two steps behind. Not a shred of doubt remained that he'd follow. When they reached the wooden stairs, her sole caught a jagged edge. Without checking over her shoulder, she flung herself backward before it could splinter her foot. Arms open, she let Bastian catch her in his strong embrace.

"Careful, *tesoro*." He whirled her around in the fresh sea breeze before setting her on her own once he made sure she could stand steady.

Tears filled her eyes as she stared into his determined expression. Though it seemed ridiculous, she knew he'd be there to catch her if she needed him but would always set her free when she craved her independence.

She swore to do the same for him, supporting his career and their relationship in whatever shape it took on. The forces of nature that had driven them together would permit nothing less.

EPILOGUE

Six months later

LynnLuvs2Trvl: Hello, ladies! I have some great news. Sebastian won his fourth world championship! Yes, that's right, we're off to celebrate with a three-month trip to Asia. Bali, here we come. I'm not sure how great the internet connection will be at the beach but don't worry, Bastian will be taking good care of me. ☺

I think this will be a great chance for us to see how things would work out if I decide to accept his proposal. I miss him so much when we're apart. I'm starting to forget why I thought it was a good idea in the first place.

So, anyone feel like visiting me in Europe next year? I think I'm going to need someone to hold my hand during the circuit events. Watching them live is scarier than on TV.

Besides… I know another hot young guy who could use a sexy Cougar.

Okay, Bastian's giving me that look. Yeah, you know the one. Gotta run, I'll write when I can!

SHIFTING GEARS

JAYNE RYLON

Dedication

To the RAW Readers group for always making my day with compliments, talk of our favorite books and lots of laughs. Can't wait to see you again!

Trademarks Acknowledgement

The author acknowledges the trademarked status and trademark owners of the following wordmarks mentioned in this work of fiction:

Angels and Airwaves: DeLonge, Thomas

iPod: Apple, Inc.

Kindle: Amazon Technologies, Inc.

National Geographic: National Geographic Society Corporation

Netflix: Netflix, Inc.

Pop-Tarts: Kellogg North America Company Corporation

U-Haul: U-Haul International, Inc.

Chapter One

"Oh my God!"

The woman on the corrugated aluminum bleacher several rows in front of Sloan turned with wide eyes when Sloan shouted. She caught Sloan's stare on the sexy cover of her erotic romance novel and flipped it closed—cover side down—discretely.

"Sorry, didn't mean to startle you." Sloan smiled. "I know how it is when you're lost in a good book. And *that* book is fan-fucking-tastic! I love that author. Her stories are smoking hot. Especially the ménages. Yum."

The woman grinned and nodded. "I've read almost all of hers. My reading group back in the US mailed me this one. It arrived last night and I'm halfway done already. I tried to ration it out—a chapter a day—but it's impossible."

"Thank God for ebook readers, huh? I don't know what I would do if I didn't have access to all the new releases from this side of the globe." Sloan stepped into the stands then picked her way down the incline, closer to the woman, careful not to slip in her three-inch heels.

At least she'd worn jeans to the race site today instead of her usual skirted suit. "I hear that. It can get lonely being a foreigner in a country where you don't speak the language. Especially one as difficult to pick up as Mandarin or Cantonese. Reading keeps me from getting too homesick, though it leads to other…

complications."

When the woman laughed, her entire face brightened. Around Sloan's age, close to forty, she seemed carefree and infectiously happy. "I know what you mean. Or, at least I used to. Now I have a young stud to keep me occupied when I get revved up. I'm engaged to Sebastian Fiori. The driver for—"

"Oh! Don't worry, I know who he is. Sexy as sin and a four-time world champion rally car racer to boot. So you must be Lynn Madison, you bitch."

The humongous diamond flashing on the woman's finger had confirmed Sloan's suspicions.

Talk of Bastian and the alluring cougar who'd tamed him had run rampant this season. Scores of young sex goddesses mourned their loss. Many had tried for years to snag him or his luscious navigator Mark Rossi, but none had succeeded in tempting either guy into more than a one-night stand.

Until Sebastian fell head over heels in love on first sight last season. Everyone agreed he'd never performed better. Lynn must be good for the man.

What was good for the driver was good for the sport.

And *that* was good for Sloan.

"It's true." Lynn sighed and her eyes took on a faraway look. "I'm the luckiest woman alive."

"I'm Sloan Desai, by the way." She held out her hand, but Lynn hugged her instead of shaking it.

"Sorry, but after two minutes I feel like I've known you forever. Have a seat." Lynn gestured with the spine of her novel toward the racetrack, which snaked past the base of the stadium they sat in. "You know, Bastian's mentioned you before. I think we might've even talked on the phone once when you scheduled some of his interviews. You're the publicist for the league, right?"

"Yep. That's me." Sloan winked. "In charge of keeping the boys out of trouble with the media, managing their images and bringing fans in by the truckload."

"Seems like you're doing a great job. I heard the first couple days of the exhibition are sold out."

"They are. Thanks."

"So how do you like China so far?"

The event would take place in Guangdong province, about a half-hour outside Guangzhou, in a few weeks—a great chance for the teams to tune up or experiment in the off-season. The crews had arrived early to acclimate, which meant Sloan had to be on-site to defuse any…situations…that could cause trouble with the local hosts.

Full of testosterone and daring, the guys in the league sometimes crossed the line.

"I haven't been able to do much sightseeing. I have to stick fairly close-by." Sloan shrugged.

"Yeah, I know what you mean." Lynn grimaced. "The teams do tend to get rowdy on occasion. Maybe you can take a day trip or two with me. I write travel guides for a living, so I like to check out as much as I can in the areas we visit. Sebastian gets nervous when I'm out on my own though. Especially in locations a little more exotic."

"You don't seem like the kind of woman to sit around and wait for a man simply to ease his mind. A woman after my own heart, by the way."

"You're right, I'm no shrinking violet." Lynn grinned. "But I worry that if *he's* worried, he'll be distracted. The sport is dangerous enough as it is. Plus, I miss him if I stray too far."

"I hope 'him' is me." A deep growl sounded from behind their spot on the bench. Sitting side by side, neither woman had heard the soft soles of Sebastian's racing sneakers on the concrete as he approached. "Or I'll have to kick some ass and those days are supposed to be behind me."

"Old man."

Sloan swallowed hard at the jibe from the other guy who strode toward them—Mark Rossi. It was either that or moan aloud at his spectacular build. Thick muscles filled out his racing jumpsuit to perfection. She wished she'd seen him going instead of coming so she could check out his killer ass, but the bulge at his crotch and the humor in his warm eyes made for scrumptious consolation prizes.

She'd spied him from across the room at events she'd arranged, but usually she had a job to do while in attendance. Of course she'd found herself staring at promo shots of him on more occasions than she cared to admit, but never before had she been able to take her time and study his legendary features in person—bold cheekbones, olive skin and glossy, sandy hair.

And, shit, now she was staring.

Maybe her imagination played tricks on her, but it seemed as if he might be gawking in return.

Sebastian coughed, the sound camouflaging something suspiciously close to a laugh when he clapped Mark between the shoulders, shoving him forward. The men ate up the remaining distance separating them from the ladies with two long strides.

"I think you all know each other. Bastian, Mark, this is Sloan Desai—the league's publicist."

"Oh yeah. Thanks for all the times you've covered my ass. *Our* asses." Sebastian shook her hand, firm but polite, before moving toward his woman. "It's nice to see you again."

"You too."

Close enough to get a very adequate view, Sloan was singed by the fire in the driver's gaze when it locked with Lynn's. Collateral damage had never felt so good. What would it be like to have that kind of intensity, sexual awareness and hunger focused on her?

The couple embraced, sharing a kiss worthy of the silver screen. Sebastian tangled his fingers in Lynn's hair then devoured her lips with eager abandon. Sloan's heart ached, her nipples tightened and a tingle ran through her body. She tore her attention from the exchange, afraid to come off like a total lecher.

Mark grinned when she spun.

Busted.

"I can't take them anywhere." He shook his head, but the curve of his delectable mouth belied his chagrin. "It's always like this. You'd think they'd been apart for months instead of two and a half hours."

"Must be nice," Sloan whispered under her breath.

After her promotion to head of the division, she'd begun touring the circuit. Instead of missing her, her husband seemed to enjoy his time alone. He'd acted inconvenienced when she returned to the States from long stretches abroad. Turned out, having her home made scheduling trysts with his slutty girlfriends troublesome. Once she'd realized the score, she divorced the loser then buried herself in work so she didn't have to admit all her childhood assumptions about romance had turned out to be false.

Hopefully Lynn and Sebastian could beat the odds.

Sloan blinked, praying Mark didn't notice the tears stinging her eyes. She peeked up at him, flinching when he canted his head and reached for her.

"I guess I'd better get going." She hustled along the concrete ramp beside the bleachers. The clicking of her heels ricocheted in the quiet space. "Really nice to meet you all. Lynn, maybe we can catch up soon. I have a stash of books in my suitcase. I finished a fabulous one by Nicole Austin last night. You're welcome to borrow it."

"Oh! You're leaving?" The other woman shook her head as she emerged from the cocoon of desire her lover had woven around them. "Why don't you come out to dinner with us?"

"No." Panic sent her heart rate skyrocketing. When the trio leveled curious stares in her direction, she softened her instinctive denial. "I have some…things…to attend to. I really can't."

"Damn. I miss having friends to chat with." Lynn seemed genuinely disappointed. "Most of the women who travel with the drivers have bigger boobs than brains and aren't very mature, if you know what I mean."

Sloan laughed. Did she ever. Constant youth and beauty surrounded the racing scene. Just one more reason she must be crazy for thinking Mark still regarded her with interest. If only she could convince her pussy to stop clenching at the idea. "Maybe we'll run into each other again soon."

Preferably sometime when the two studs didn't incite her hormones to rampage and the palpable love in the air didn't aggravate her bruised heart.

"Wait!" Lynn stopped Sloan again when she would have bolted in a dignified yet hasty escape. "Here, take this."

The woman dug through her purse, scribbled something on the back of a receipt then handed the slip of paper to Sebastian who passed it to Mark. His warm fingers grazed hers when he pressed the note into her palm. Holy crap. She had to get out of there before she melted. The tropical sun and the Italian stallion scorched her insides.

"What is it?" Sloan glanced at the bubbly script.

"A web address. For a blog my friends and I keep to talk about our favorite books. You know, the juicy ones. Hop online and chat with us."

"Ah, sure. I'll do that." Her face flamed when she realized Lynn had outted her love of erotic romance to two of the hottest men on earth. "I'll check it out tonight. Nice to meet you all."

"You too." Sebastian graced her with one of his infamous smiles.

She intended to settle for a finger wave before she spun on her heel, but Mark snatched her hand in his and raised it to his lips. Moist warmth bussed her knuckles, weakening her knees.

"The pleasure was mine." He winked to offset some of his stuffy formality.

She had to laugh at his audacity and cheesy imitation of seduction that somehow still managed to unleash butterflies in her stomach. At least she didn't have to pretend to take him seriously.

"See you soon." He held Sloan's gaze long enough that she thought she might drown in his deep, chocolate eyes before returning to his friends with one last glimpse over his sturdy shoulder.

* * * * *

Sloan used one long, red fingernail to click the X in the top corner of her mail program, work complete for the night. So what if it was after midnight local time? She often put in ridiculous hours.

What else did she have to do these days?

Maybe she'd download a new book to read before bed, something sexy and a little naughty—a novel about an older woman and a younger man sounded fantastic.

Who was she kidding?

Ever since she'd run into Mark Rossi, he was all she could think about. When she'd found herself accessing the crew bio files earlier, she'd checked his birthday. At forty-one to his twenty-nine, there was a significant gap between them.

Insane. But his friends made the disparity work for them. Watching the pair interact had left her no doubt of their true, undying love for each other—a rare thing in the world today. No way could Sloan muster that kind of luck.

Still, it wouldn't hurt anything to take Lynn up on the offer to join her book club. It *had* been fun to discuss the stories they both enjoyed. Most of the time Sloan kept them out of sight. The racy covers wouldn't have helped her obtain or maintain her position in a man's sport. She even made sure to lock her Kindle when she finished sneaking a chapter or two during her lunch breaks or while waiting for an evening event, although none of her clients had ever expressed interest in her pastime other than to tease her for her bookworm tendencies. They probably thought she read biographies, poignant non-fiction or trendy economic postulations.

Hell, if nothing else, Lynn's friends could probably give Sloan a suggestion or two on her late-night purchase—ensure she bought a book she'd really enjoy.

She reached across the stylish bamboo desk in her apartment for her briefcase. It still awed her that a modest monthly rent bought such a lavish living space, complete with daily maid service, in this area. Parquet floors, marble counters and air conditioning in every room made this one of the most luxurious places she'd stayed abroad since recent budget cuts had scaled back on executive frivolity. Even the lush bed spoke of decadence in a country where thin, stiff pallets were preferred to squishy mattresses capped with feather pillow-tops.

Sloan dug the scrap of paper from the outside pocket of her bag then typed in the URL Lynn had scribbled.

http://tempthecougar.blogspot.com/

Holy Hannah. She hadn't looked at the address closely enough. This was no ordinary group of friends who shared reading recommendations and mooned over their favorite heroes.

No, this was a collection of women who'd taken things to the next level.

Sloan scanned their homepage. From the tantalizing man splayed across the blog's header, through the confessional posts of older women on the prowl, past scores of erotic romance novel reviews and photos of sexy men, to the appreciative thanks of friends who'd gotten support on their personal adventures, the revelations inspired her.

She felt as though she'd invaded these women's diaries, but she couldn't pry her stare from the screen of her laptop.

From what she pieced together, the original friends had met at a romance readers' convention then made a pact to each hunt up a willing younger partner—or two—for a wild affair. They called it the Cougar Challenge. And fuck if it didn't look as if most had gotten more than they bargained for.

Love along with lust.

Just like Lynn and Sebastian.

How many women had taken the Cougar Challenge? How many were living their dreams?

After the intimate peek into their lives, it didn't feel right to leave without introducing herself. Besides, if she were honest, she envied them. It couldn't hurt to learn more about their successes.

Sloan: Knock, knock. Hi there. I'm Sloan and I love dirty books. ☺ I ran into Lynn this afternoon and she ratted you all out, giving me the address for the *Tempt the Cougar* blog. I've been lurking, catching up on some of the posts. I have to say I'm impressed! You ladies are daring and unbelievably lucky to have scored such amazing, young men. And these pictures! Wow, where'd you find so many hotties? Can you send one my way?

By the time she clicked send, her clock glowed a horrifying two a.m. At least tomorrow was Saturday. If everyone behaved themselves, she wouldn't have to work.

This late she didn't expect any responses. At midday in the US, most of the Cougar women would be at work. But, as she switched windows to browse her favorite bookseller, a digital ping alerted her to a new post. Then another and another until the window lit up like a Christmas tree and the comments kept rolling in.

Apparently the Cougar women were serious about their

blogging.

Lori: Hey Sloan! So glad you could join us at *Tempt the Cougar*. Ya know, I think we all love naughty books. Wonder if there's a twelve-step program for that? Hmm. If you hang around with us long enough, you are bound to be corrupted, but what a wonderful way to sin!

Lynn: Sloan! Welcome to the group. I know a guy who'd make the perfect Cougar bait for you. Don't think I didn't notice you and Mark checking each other out.

Autumn: Hi Sloan, a big welcome. You'll love taking the Cougar Challenge. Sounds like you've already got eyes on a hot young stud. I say go for it. The rewards are totally excellent.

Sloan: What are you doing up this time of night, Lynn? And…well…I may have been drooling on Mark, as embarrassing as that is to admit, but I doubt it went any further than that.

Lynn: Want me to ask him? He's sitting on the couch next to me. He and Bastian are arguing about optimal fuel mixes and suspension systems right now. Blech. If I give him your number, we'll all be happy. He'll be out of here faster than their world record pace and I can put Sebastian to bed right.

Cam: Sloan! Welcome. ☺ And hey now, some details about the chemistry!!!

Sloan: No, Lynn, don't ask Mark anything! And sorry, no details, Cam. There's nothing to tell.

Lynn: Maybe not yet, but, Cougars, you should have seen how his eyes almost bugged out of his skull when he saw Sloan. I guarantee he wants her.

Sloan: Ugg! I hope he can't see your screen.

Rachel: Ohhhh, I hope he can. Nice to "meet" you, by the way. I'm glad Lynn has some company over there. Give her a hug for me next time you see her, okay?

Sloan: Nice to meet you too. And sure. But please don't encourage her. I've had about as much rejection as I can stomach lately.

Rachel: Sorry, hon, that doesn't sound like good news.

Why not let Mark cheer you up? Be your rebound guy? It doesn't have to be about forever. Start with one hot night. I've heard he's more than capable…

Lynn: Rachel! Zip it!

Sloan: Now that sounds interesting.

Before Sloan could delve more into the innuendo, the rest of the Cougar ladies were off to the races, setting her and Mark up on some imaginary Challenge-fulfilling date. The busybodies had her cracking up while about to pull her hair out. She loved them—and feared them—already.

Stevie: Welcome Sloan! We have a ball around here. If you like the young ones, this is the place to be. As for the Challenge, it was the best thing that ever happened to me. Go ahead, do it. I dare ya! You won't regret it.

Lynn: Give me your phone number and I'll let Mark tell you the dirt.

Sloan: I don't know if that's a good idea…

Rachel: As an impartial observer, I guarantee it is. It's a great idea. You can thank me later. And, I officially double dare you to take the Cougar Challenge.

Sloan: Maybe I'll work up to that.

Elizabeth: Hey Sloan! Just do it. Suffice it to say, not one of us has regretted taking the Challenge. Question is, will you regret it if you don't?

Lynn: Make that a triple dog dare.

Sloan: Holy crap! You ladies should be gnats, not Cougars! ☺ Okay, okay, I'm emailing it to you now. It's not like he's going to call, sorry to disappoint you all.

Lynn: Looks like he and Bastian are wrapping up for the night or should I say morning. But I'm still giving him your number. Don't be surprised!

Sloan: Somehow I doubt he'll use it. Anyway, how about you and I meet up again soon? Dinner tomorrow night? At Yunnan's. Six o'clock. I'll bring the latest Lexxie Couper book!

Lynn: Damn, I'm easy. Sure. See you then.

Sloan: Good night, ladies, thanks for the laughs. Can't

wait to chat more when I'm fully awake.

Rachel: Nice to meet you! Talk to you soon! Then we can say "we told you so"!

A grin still lingered as Sloan stripped off her gown, settling onto the cool sheets of her crisply made bed. It always felt more comfortable when someone else had done the work.

She checked her phone.

Nope, not on silent mode.

She sighed and rolled her eyes at herself when a hint of disappointment tinged her amusement with her newfound friends.

Of course Mark hadn't called. Silly of her to let the wild ladies on the blog get her hopes up. But the idea would make for some spectacular dreams.

Her eyelids drifted shut, her mind blanked and a soft smile curved her lips as she crept toward sleep, but images of Mark kept returning to her imagination. The fuzzy material of her covers brushed her beaded nipples, making her squirm. The motion highlighted the dampness on her thighs.

Shit, no way could she fall asleep like this.

Sloan's fingers meandered along the top of her trim leg, across her flat tummy to her breast. For a woman in her forties, she thought she still looked pretty damn fine. She cupped the supple weight, rubbing some of the ache from her nipple. Her other hand wandered toward her pussy. A moan escaped her and her hips lifted toward the fingertips intended to soothe the pressure building in her swollen mound.

What if Mark were here? Would he allow her to slake her building desire? Would he enjoy being ridden? Would he fit her well?

The thought inspired her to slip one finger through the slick moisture around her clit and rub the swollen flesh.

And then her phone rang.

Chapter Two

An obnoxious ringtone cut into her fantasy. How many times had it gone off before she'd noticed? Reflexes drove her to answer. Fast.

Sloan lunged for the display blinking in the darkness. *Please, God, don't let it switch to voicemail. Don't let me miss Mark's call.*

If she hadn't worked herself into a horny frenzy, maybe she would have considered the consequences of that wish awhile longer. Instead, she ripped open the phone and panted, "Hello?"

"Uh…"

Oh crap. It must sound as if a frog had crawled in her throat and died.

"Sloan? You there?" Mark sounded a little sleepy and a lot sexy. Could he guess what she'd been up to? Had he been thinking along the same lines?

"Yeah." She bit her lip, wondering if she should apologize or pretend to be oblivious. Denial ruled as a first line of defense in her business dealings so she stuck with what came natural. "Good morning."

"Sorry, were you sleeping?" He acted as if there were nothing odd about calling a woman in the dead of night. "Lynn told me you were awake. I wasn't going to bother you so late but I…uh…couldn't sleep. Should I call back tomorrow?"

"No!" The objection sounded more like a shout than a relaxed denial. "I mean, this is fine."

"Sloan?" His tone morphed into something dangerous, something intoxicating.

"Mark?" She wished she could see his melted-chocolate eyes. All of him, for that matter. He was supremely lickable.

"Can we cut the shit?"

He surprised a chuckle out of her. After the pile of lies she'd waded through with her ex-husband, Mark's directness came as a welcome relief. Besides, she'd long since outgrown the dating game. A man didn't call close to three o'clock in the morning to say hello. "I would like that very much."

"I'm lying in bed with a hard-on the size of the leaning tower of Pisa in my shorts because I can't stop thinking about you." He cursed under his breath, his Italian accent far more distinguishable in the sultry summer night. "Ever since we bumped into you, I've been wondering about the sparks between us. Do you like all the spicy things you read about? Are you as sexy under that all-business exterior as I think? I can't help imagining all the fun we could have together."

He paused, but his candor had her so turned-on she couldn't form a response.

"Say something. Tell me it's the same for you or tell me to get lost. No hard feelings."

"It's not exactly the same," she whispered, enjoying teasing him for a few seconds.

"Shit, *scusi*. I'll go—"

"I mean, I don't have a hard-on anywhere near me." Where the hell had she found the courage to say that? The Cougars were to blame. They'd put all sorts of daring ideas in her mind. "But I wish I did."

"Thank you, *Dio*." His voice turned rougher, gravelly. "You sounded...hungry when you answered my call. Were you touching yourself?"

"Yes." She licked her lips then decided if they were going to be naughty, she should commit one hundred percent to the experience. It's wasn't as though she'd ever do it again after tonight. "I still am."

Sloan set the phone on speaker then dropped it to the pillow beside her head. She caressed herself from her neck to her hips, stroking every inch of supple skin. A soft whimper floated from her parted lips.

"Beautiful." Mark groaned on the other end of the line. "I've always thought you were hot as hell. But you were married, weren't you?"

Her arousal cooled as though someone had doused her with cold water. "Yes."

"Damn it. I shouldn't have asked." He forced the statement through gritted teeth. "It doesn't matter. But I can't believe I didn't notice you were available."

"I wasn't." She didn't intend to lead him on. "I still might not be. I haven't tried this since—"

"Damn, I don't mean to drag you down. Let me make it up to you. Can I bring you breakfast in bed?"

"Maybe later." She decided to reclaim her buzz one way or the other. And the temptation of an Italian stallion like Mark at her disposal made for a powerful aphrodisiac. He'd called, willing to help her fulfill the Cougar Challenge. She didn't want to squander the opportunity, not when she had the perfect excuse to take what she needed. "First, I want you to take your clothes off. Get naked for me."

"Shit, yes." Rustling echoed out of the speaker. "You don't mess around. I like that about you."

"I'm glad." Sloan grinned in the darkness. She teased the rosy area around her nipples until they contracted once more. "Besides, you were overdressed. No reason I should be the only one nude."

"You're naked? Really?"

"Yes, really." She loved the awe in his tone. "I always sleep in the buff."

"Mmm." He sighed. "We'll have to have a slumber party sometime. Soon."

"Maybe, if there's no real slumber involved." Sloan found that once she'd released her inner Cougar, she couldn't trap it in its cage again.

"I promise," he growled. "Sloan?"

"Yes, Mark?" She purred when she pinched her nipples.

"Tell me what to do."

"Wrap your hand around your cock." She'd never given a

man orders before, but she found it suited her. The resulting moan from his end of the phone went a long way toward rekindling her desire. "Now talk to me. What does it feel like?"

"Christ, it's hard. So hard. And slippery. Feels hot, heavy." His breathing hitched as he explored for her. "The ridge around the tip is bulging. Let me stroke it."

"Not yet."

He hissed a breath and she pictured him with his jaw clenched, one hand fisted at his side.

"Cup your balls with your other hand."

"That makes my cock jerk. I can feel my sac expanding and contracting."

His matter-of-fact narration certainly didn't keep her calm. In fact, exactly the opposite was true. Lynn shifted on the bed, spreading her legs wide apart.

"I wish I could find out for myself. Wish I could take you inside me." Sloan dipped one finger inside her soaked pussy. He'd stretch her. She couldn't remember the last time she'd had sex. Never mind great sex. Pitiful.

"You can. Tell me where you are. Let me come to you."

"Not this time." She wasn't ready to give up their game yet. "But you can come *with* me."

"Does that mean you're touching yourself again?"

"Mmm...yes." She closed her eyes as she rubbed her clit.

"Put the phone between your legs. Let me hear how wet you are." His request ensured she reached new levels of arousal.

With one hand, she held the phone while she used the other to fuck herself. The wet slurps and sucking sounds would have horrified old Sloan, but this new, adventurous Cougar went for it. She settled her hand deeper, moved it faster and increased the offering until Mark shouted over the phone, "*Dio!* I bet you taste amazing."

Sloan placed the device back on the pillow with a sigh.

"If I were there, I'd lick you clean before burying my cock in all that silky heat."

The mental image he painted of his tawny hair between her thighs sabotaged her plans to draw out their pleasure. "Go ahead, jerk yourself. Slow. All the way from the base to the tip."

Sloan gave him a few seconds to settle himself then asked,

"Did you get any cream on your hand?"

"Yeah." He cursed. "Impossible not to at this point. I've been hard all day. I'm leaking like a broken faucet here."

"Taste yourself."

"Uh, Sloan, I've never done that…" He hesitated.

When she refused to let him off the hook, he caved.

"But if it turns you on, I'll try it. I'm pretty open-minded. I'll do whatever you like. Just don't stop touching yourself."

She listened hard enough she could have heard a pin drop—until something better reached her ears. His lips smacked around his salty, cum-coated fingers. "Damn, that's kind of hot."

Sloan agreed. She whimpered as she teased herself higher, closer toward the finish line promising satisfaction. "The thought of two guys together always turns me on. Have you ever fooled around with another man? Would you?"

She hadn't intended for the questions to come out. They hardly knew each other yet she'd already revealed her inner freak! But she'd taken their joint insanity this far, so why hedge now? Besides, she was experimenting with brutal honesty. It was time to go for what she really wanted. No more worrying about everyone else's needs.

"Never have. But would I? I-I don't know." Mark grunted. She could tell from his breathing that he worked himself faster now. "I would have said 'absolutely not' until recently. But something happened, with Lynn and Sebastian. Maybe. I might try it. If it was with the right person."

A sudden contraction gripped her, making her moan loudly.

"You like the idea, Sloan?"

"So much." She inserted another finger in her gripping channel. "Tell me about the change of heart. Lynn said you'd share if I gave you my number."

"We had a threesome. Sebastian, Lynn and I." He breathed hard between his sentences now. "Actually, Bastian and I have shared women a bunch of times. But never anything between us. Unless you count touching by accident when we fucked the same girls."

A gasp interrupted his retelling. She used the hand not tunneling inside her pussy to rub tiny circles around her clit. It wouldn't take much more.

"The last time, we were with Lynn. She rode Sebastian—reverse cowgirl—while I ate her pussy. *Dio*, she tasted so fucking good. But not half as good as I bet you would."

"Flattery." It was all she could manage.

The story he told captured her full attention. The rippling walls of her pussy squeezed her fingers tighter as she imagined what it would be like to be the center of that much male attention. Delicious.

He surrendered a short bark of laughter before continuing. "While I worked on her, she insisted I put my finger in Sebastian's ass. I liked it. Enough that, once things got hot and heavy, I lost it and pumped my spunk all down his leg. Shit. My best damn friend."

Sloan couldn't catch her breath enough to attempt a response.

She closed her eyes and imagined the shocked look on Mark's face as he emptied his balls all over the furred shin of his driver. And that was all it took.

"Oh God. Mark!" She screamed when she came, shuddering and tensing so hard she got a cramp in her curled toes.

"Yes, come, Sloan. Come." He shouted, a raw and base command tinting his voice. "I'm coming…with you."

The knowledge spiked her ecstasy higher, prolonging her release. Damn, the man loved to talk. And talk dirty.

"Shot all over my chest. My abs. Some splashed over my nipple."

She kept rubbing her clit, wringing every last drop of satisfaction from her orgasm and his confession.

"Taste it. For me." Her voice trembled. "Imagine it's Sebastian's come instead of yours."

"Fuck yes." A wet slurp followed, setting off another mini-orgasm in her core.

Mark murmured reassurances for long minutes as she recovered, finally floating back to earth and the welcome embrace of his husky voice.

"Thank you."

"No, thank *you*. Sloan, tell me where you are. I want to look into your eyes when we talk about what just happened and what might come next. I'll steal you a packet of Pop-Tarts from Lynn's stash of American snacks if you require more bribing."

"Oh my God. She has Pop-Tarts?" With the global marketplace, some hints of home seemed universal but others were difficult to procure outside Hong Kong, Guangzhou or the other metropolitan areas nearby.

"Strawberry *and* blueberry. There might even be a few of the brown sugar kind left."

"Marco Rossi, I think I'm in love with you."

"I know the feeling. But you must have been peeking at my official paperwork. Only my *mamma* calls me Marco. And I definitely don't think of you like my mother."

"I'm probably old enough to be—"

His raucous laughter cut her off. "Don't be ridiculous."

"No matter how I acted tonight, I'm no racing groupie. That's for sure."

"Sloan?"

"Yeah." She hesitated, her finger a fraction of an inch from the button that would end their call. Now that they'd eased some of their sexual tension, would he cut and run?

"*When* I get there…I don't want you to think I'm assuming anything. Things got a little crazy tonight, but I'm not expecting more…physical stuff. You know, sex. I don't want to scare you away. I won't touch you if you're not ready. We can talk. Really talk. Figure out where this is headed."

"Once a navigator, always a navigator."

She smiled when he laughed at her lame joke before persisting, "Yeah, so where are you staying? Tell me."

"Same building as you. Apartment 3027."

"Isn't that right down the hall?"

"Uh-huh."

"So why the telefuck?" He choked on another laugh. "Not that I didn't enjoy it."

Sloan shrugged though he couldn't see it. "It was fun."

And safe.

But it only made her crave more—the comfort of another human's contact. Intimacy she hadn't known in forever. "Marco, what if I *need* you to touch me?"

"I'll be right there."

Dead air followed.

Sloan giggled as she burrowed into her pillows, sated and

elated at the same time.

Not two minutes later a knock sounded at the door. She practically skipped to the other room, put her eye to the peep hole then busted out laughing.

"Let me in, quick."

She flung open the polished wood, a naked Marco zipping past her. She relocked the door then turned when she heard a crinkle. He held a plastic packet for her approval. "Would have been here even faster but I didn't want to skip out on my promise of snackage. Good thing Bastian and I have connecting rooms. Though I think I knocked their coffee table over in the dark. Maybe they won't notice?"

"What if someone had been in the hallway? You could have taken two seconds to throw on some clothes, I'm not going anywhere."

"At this time of night, they'd probably be too drunk to remember tomorrow. I didn't want to take the chance you'd change your mind."

Sloan let her gaze wander from his movie-star face, along his sculpted body to his cock—impressive even half-hard—then back to his eyes, which made their own appraising circuit of her nude form. Somehow she didn't feel the least bit self-conscious.

"You don't need to worry about me changing my mind." She took the silver package from his hand and set it on the table.

"Not hungry?" He frowned a little.

"Not for junk food. Except maybe beefcake." Sloan closed the gap between them and devoured his lips. Their arms entwined around each other—necks, backs, waists—in a flurry of desperate embraces. Her torso brushed his, still sticky from his recent climax.

"You feel amazing in my arms." He mumbled between nips on her neck. "And yeah, I might not be thirty yet, but you're still going to have to give me a couple minutes to recover. You destroyed me on the phone. Plus…"

She raised her gaze to his, amused by the wonder there.

"I can't believe I'm about to say this. A first, I swear." He took a tiny step backward. "I want to talk. I sort of promised myself no more meaningless sex."

"With me or in general?" Sloan held out her hand and he

accepted it. She led him to her bed then climbed in. He followed but sat, his shoulders resting against the headboard, instead of snuggling next to her.

"I guess I realized I was never going to find what Bastian and Lynn have if I keep running around like a kid, fucking beautiful women who aren't important to me."

Sloan's eyebrows rose. "So you're looking for something permanent?"

"You're not?"

"Marco, I was married. Things went to hell. I don't think I'm ready to sacrifice like that again. Might never be." She rolled to her back then rubbed her eyes, surprised when he tucked the covers over her exposed breasts as though the sight made it difficult for him to think or have a serious conversation. "I thought the Cougar Challenge was about having a good time, that's all."

"What the fuck is the Cougar Challenge?"

The ice in his tone had her bolting upright, dragging the sheet with her. "Oh crap. I thought Lynn put you up to this! She told me to jump onboard the bandwagon like the rest of her friends. They dared me to hook up with a younger man…you…for a night of fun. Why the hell did you call me if you didn't know I was a guaranteed lay?"

"Wait. You're saying Lynn *dared* you to fuck me? Lynn—Sebastian's Lynn?"

"Shit, shit, shit." Sloan's mouth dropped open at the anger darkening his eyes. "I thought you knew. When she gave you my number—"

"So, what, this was some scheme cooked up by a group of horny older women?" He jumped to his feet. "Any young stud with a hard cock would do?"

"No, Marco—"

"Don't call me that." He shrugged off her touch then marched into the bathroom.

When he returned with a towel wrapped around his waist, she started to hide her face in her hands to avoid the accusation in his glare then decided those days were long gone. "*You* called *me*! You started in on the dirty talk practically before you said hello."

"Because I've had some lame school-kid crush on you for

years. I'm sure you don't remember. You'd have had to see me for that. Everyone notices Sebastian, not me. I'm just the navigator. Some loser who rides along with a superstar and drools over smoking-hot professional ladies who are completely out of my league unless they decide to slum it with some young, dumb, walking hard-on for a night of endless fucking."

She tried to refute his self-deprecating claims but nothing would come out of her stunned throat except a choked gurgle. Not that he would have heard her over the vicious string of Italian that she'd bet her life contained more curses than anything else.

"Why the hell should you be any different? I always dreamed of a chance with you. I thought divine intervention, or at least poetic justice, made sure you'd be the first woman I tried for more with. Of course, guys who want a girlfriend don't call her and start jerking off over the phone two minutes later. *Dio!*"

"Because you did…I assumed you knew." Sloan swallowed hard at the disbelief etching lines around his sexy mouth. "I'm sorry."

She clambered to her knees at the foot of the bed and reached for him, to run a soothing hand along the bunched muscles of his shoulder, but he evaded her.

"I would never have used you like that." Horror churned her stomach.

"Yeah, well, sorry you didn't get your fill." He strode from the room. "I can send one of the other crew members over if you're still horny. I'm sure any of them would like to take your *Challenge*. Maybe you could screw a few at once, really show the rest of your friends up?"

Before she could object, he'd slammed the door hard enough to knock the package of pastries onto the floor. Shattered.

Tears streamed from her eyes in stunned silence. How had things gone from sugar to shit so fast? She should have known better. Relationships always ended this way. Even the one-night-stand variety.

She wouldn't forget it again.

And judging by the arguing echoing down the hall, from the direction of Lynn and Sebastian's apartment, she thought she might have ruined some friendships in her disastrous attempt at a no-strings affair.

Sloan couldn't bear to listen to the fallout. She headed for her shower to drown the noise and attempt to cleanse herself of the disgust making her feel dirty. Dirtier than the night she'd discovered the bed she'd slept in for years had hosted dozens of other women while she was out of town.

This time she'd been the villain at fault.

Chapter Three

Sloan ignored yet another notification of a post on the *Tempt the Cougar* blog. She'd tried to unsubscribe from the damn feed but it seemed like the administrator wasn't responding or her computer had joined the plot to make her life miserable.

She'd spent the day moping in bed watching Chinese television—with no subtitles. What she wouldn't give for Netflix and a queue full of romantic comedies right now.

After avoiding the Cougar site all afternoon, she surrendered. Otherwise, she'd have no choice but to keep her dinner appointment with Lynn, who refused to confirm her cancellation text messages. Damn it.

She skimmed past Lynn's lengthy apology and the rest of the Cougars checking in to see if both of them had survived the day intact. If she read their reassurances or encouragement she'd start to cry again, and she'd sworn she'd done enough of that to last a lifetime.

Still, the most recent message caught her eye.

Lynn: Sloan, this is all my fault. I should have been more clear with Mark. I have to interview a local travel agent this afternoon but I'll be waiting for you tonight as planned. Please come. Let me make it up to you. I have a brand new Desiree Holt novel set aside for you. It's autographed.

Well shit. Now she had to go. Because it wasn't fair to make Lynn shoulder the entire burden of this fiasco. The woman had tried to help her out, fix her up. It wasn't Lynn's fault Sloan had the inverse Midas touch. A constant black cloud hovered over her head and her love life.

Plus, she adored Desiree Holt.

At least she'd have something to read during the long, lonely nights ahead. Funny, she hadn't recognized the suffocating silence in the room, and her life, until Mark had filled it with his laughter and desire. Even for a moment. Like a flash of lightning, his companionship had illuminated all the flaws in her current existence then disappeared, leaving her in the dark once more.

Crap.

* * * * *

Sloan tapped her nails on the table in an incessant tattoo that did nothing to soothe her nerves. A waiter approached but she didn't have the energy to butcher what little Cantonese she'd been able to absorb. Instead, she pointed to the wine list at the bottom of the laminated menu then held up two fingers. It would take more than one glass of white zin to settle her nerves.

Luckily "Thank you" was pretty universal.

She'd already drained both and most of a third on an empty stomach when a pair of platform heels she'd kill for entered her field of vision as she studied the ground. The intricate pattern on the carpet started to make her dizzy.

When two more pairs of shoes joined the sexy stilettos—these much bigger and sneaker-ish—Sloan jerked her gaze upward.

"Oh no." She shied away from the accusatory glare she expected from Mark, focusing on Lynn instead. "You brought the Cougar bait?"

"They insisted, sorry." Lynn didn't wait to be invited, she leaned in and hugged Sloan. "About everything. I really screwed this all up."

"S'okay." Oops, maybe she should have sipped the drinks

instead of chugging them. "You meaned—meant well."

"Let me make it right. Please talk to Mark. Hear him out. Sebastian and I will hang out at the bar for a while and, if you're up to it, the four of us can have dinner together in a little bit. Sound good?"

When Sloan nodded, the world spun. She grabbed the edge of the table in a white-knuckled grip and closed her eyes. Ah, it was better if she didn't have to try to resist the temptation of looking toward Mark. He'd make any woman dizzy.

"If you don't mind, would you put in an order now? Looks like Sloan could use some food." The anger she expected to ruin his baritone was nowhere to be found. Unlike last night, his Mediterranean accent made all his words sound as rich as dark coffee.

"We'll do that."

Sloan peeked through slit eyelids in time to catch a glimpse of Sebastian putting his arm around Lynn as he turned her toward the bar.

"Back in a few minutes. With some appetizers."

She scooted over when Mark joined her on the bench seat of the booth—on her side of the table. She kept moving until her arm encountered the wall, but Mark pursued her until their thighs pressed together from hips to knees. He was so warm he melted her insides.

Or maybe the wine did that.

"Are you okay?" His question struck her as absurd and she giggled.

Then suddenly she couldn't stop. One laugh became a riot of chuckles. She had no hope of restraining her nerves or the ridiculousness of the situation. After a minute, she wiped tears from her cheeks then clenched her aching side, doubled over as far as she could go behind the table.

When she paused to draw a breath, she realized he laughed right along with her. They did seem to share the same twisted sense of humor. "Sorry, Cougar. Dumb question."

Sloan flinched at the title but couldn't help turning toward the man who'd destroyed her inhibitions with one tiny phone call and a sprinkle of dirty revelations. When she did, she gasped.

"What happened to your face?" She traced the inflamed area

slicing through his eyebrow and the bruise on his jaw with featherlight touches.

"Bastian objected to the way I chastised his woman last night." Mark grinned, the motion almost reopening a little cut on the corner of his mouth. "He shoved me and warned me to stand down, but I was all too willing to go a round or two. It's been awhile since we resorted to a good fist fight."

Sometimes she forgot how young they were. Still, his silly smirk infected her.

"Did you work it out with Lynn, or did you and Sebastian hammer each other until you ran out of steam?" She hated to bring it up and squash the easy banter between them but she had to know.

"Things are good now. With Lynn and Bastian." He scrubbed his knuckles over his eye then winced when he irritated the puffy area. "It was a miscommunication. She tried to tell me. But I only heard what I wanted to. Look, Sloan, you didn't do anything wrong. I was an asshole last night. I've hooked up with women plenty of times. You're an adult—a gorgeous, mature woman. You can fuck who you like, when you like without looking for more. It was screwed up of me to imply otherwise. I just… I'd hoped…"

"And now you've made me hope too." She couldn't believe she'd whispered her confession aloud. "Asshole."

The smile on his face was worth the potential hazards. "Really?"

Sloan nodded then reached up to kiss his injured lip. "And I'm still sorry things happened this way. Not exactly a perfect beginning for us."

"Can we start over?" He plucked her hand from her lap and traced the ridge of her knuckles with his thumb. "Lynn is planning one of her day trips tomorrow. Since we always try to take Sunday off, Sebastian and I intend to go with her. To Cheung Chau island. Off the coast, near Hong Kong. It's supposed to be beautiful. Top-notch seafood too."

"Are you asking me on a date?"

"Uh, yeah. A double date. Is that too weird, considering…?"

"Not at all." Sloan couldn't believe he still had any interest untainted.

"Psst." Lynn hesitated at the edge of the booth. "Is it okay if we have a seat?"

"Sure." Mark nodded at Sebastian. The other man set a platter of fried rice on the table before the couple slid onto the opposite bench. "I was trying to persuade Sloan to go to Cheung Chau with us tomorrow. Why don't you give it a try?"

"Great beaches, a world-renown fish market, souvenir shopping and a pirate's cave! What's not to love? You don't want to miss it." Lynn wiggled her eyebrows in an attempt to lure Sloan that set off another round of laughter.

"I'd really like to go with you." She trained her stare on the equally dinged face of the race car driver across from her. "But Sebastian better watch his step. If he lays a hand on my guy again, I'll have something to say about it."

Only after the words had flown from her lips did she think of Mark's confession the night before. Then she wished she could retrieve the jest but it was too late.

The four of them exchanged a slew of awkward glances then burst out laughing. "Let's strike that one from the record, huh?"

"Sounds great." Sloan reached up to kiss Mark's cheek. "Thank you. For being so understanding about…everything."

"And on that note, this is for you." Lynn handed a book, wrapped in pink ribbon, across the table.

"You didn't have to do this."

"I know, but I wanted to." The other woman snuggled into Sebastian's chest then sighed. "It's the least I could do."

"I appreciate it." Before Sloan could elaborate, servers delivered family style platters of steaming noodles and fresh stir-fried vegetables to their table. "This looks delicious."

"Dig in." Sebastian handed her a plate with a wink before reaching across to spoon some of the food onto his own china.

The next several hours passed in a flurry of laughter, great food, smooth wine and a failed experiment in using chopsticks. Mark fed her from his instead. Captivating conversation, interspersed with several rounds of story-telling, gave her more and more insight into her new friends.

During one particularly colorful retelling about Sebastian getting caught with his pants down—literally—which made Sloan hope no one else spoke English, the driver winged a piece of carrot across the table at Mark. The guys escalated the battle until Lynn stepped in and got caught in the crossfire.

She picked a pea from her hair while wrinkling her nose, but Sebastian took the opportunity to mock their alpha display from the night before. "Careful there, *Marco*, or you'll be going down again."

"If I remember correctly, you were the one who went down first, Bastian."

"You'd like that wouldn't you, *amico*?"

Lynn and Sloan's wide-eyed stares met across the table in a flash. Thank God she wasn't the only one who'd caught the undercurrent. She wondered if the men knew both her and Lynn frequently read books involving male-on-male interaction. Some of the bisexual ménage stories were her all-time favorites. After browsing Lynn's to-be-read list on the blog, Sloan knew the other woman enjoyed the genre as much as she did.

"I might like it." Mark chuckled, breaking the tension. "But not as much as you, fuckwad."

With that, the duo flitted off to another topic. Another crazy story. Another adventure.

Each thing she learned about the trio improved her opinion of them and highlighted the unique bond they shared. By the time Lynn kicked back in the seat, reclining against her fiancé's broad chest, her eyelids drooping, Sloan could commiserate.

The emotional roller coaster she'd ridden all day had sapped her energy.

Mark turned to her and caught her stifling a yawn behind her cupped palm. He smiled then looped his arm over her shoulders as though it were nothing—a gesture he'd made a million times before.

Physical connection came so naturally around him. She and her ex had been coworkers long before they'd become lovers. Her respect for his aptitude on the job had led to her accepting a business lunch invitation though she'd refused to see him socially. Once she'd left her company, lured away by the racing league, she agreed to take their relationship further.

They'd become acquaintances during that time and she hadn't wanted to lose their connection. She should have quickly realized the error of that logic. If he would have drifted away as a friend, clearly nothing more glued them together. Though they'd always had plenty to talk about when it came to PR, intimacy had never come easy.

Lovemaking had been quick and awkward, pleasant at best.

Looking back, she realized the dickhead had coveted her success and started lashing out with affairs around the time she really began to climb the corporate ladder. He'd used her guilt over her long hours and time away to justify his behavior. The first time she found out he'd cheated, she made an effort to repair their relationship. The next time, she left—only realizing the magnitude of his philandering when he threw it in her face during the divorce proceedings.

"What's that sigh for?" Mark whispered into her hair.

The nuzzle of his stubbled jaw condensed her nipples and made her eager to cuddle closer.

"Thinking about how effortless this is." Sloan admitted the truth to them both. She'd never felt this pure, elemental attraction to another man, certainly not her ex. She went with it, tipping her cheek onto Mark's shoulder and breathing deep. The scent of his skin mixed with his aftershave went to her head quicker than the alcohol she'd consumed earlier.

Mark squeezed her thigh beneath the table and she knew he understood.

A couple minutes later, the wait staff began stacking chairs—upside-down—on the tables around them. When had the restaurant cleared out?

"Looks like we're getting the ol' heave-ho." Sebastian smiled at her and Mark. "Lynn and I are going to walk down to the river. You're welcome to join us but I realize neither of you got much sleep last night. Are you heading back to the apartment complex?"

"Uh, yeah, I'm beat. And I assume we're leaving early in the morning." Did going home imply Mark would stay with her or in his apartment instead? Out of her league when it came to dating, especially around these two pros, she stumbled over the next move. "Where should I meet you all?"

"Don't worry, I'll take care of everything." Mark slipped from beneath her and rose to his feet, extending his hand to help her up.

That sounded promising.

Now she had to decide if she was ready to expose herself again. After an entire evening of enduring the waves of lust rolling off Mark, battering her senses, she thought she might welcome the relief.

Chapter Four

Sloan exited the taxi in front of Mark, treating him to a view worth every penny of the cab fare. Her classy pencil skirt hugged the gentle curve of her hips and snugged to her perfect ass as though the fabric had been custom cut for it. Hell, maybe it had been.

He dug in his pocket for his wallet, catching the driver stealing a peek in the rearview mirror. Well, it wasn't as if he could blame the guy. Still, his hackles rose and he stifled the urge to growl at the lucky bastard.

Enjoy the tip, buddy.

He exited the cab and reclaimed Sloan's hand, but neither one of them spoke as they headed for the elaborate entrance to their complex. The easy camaraderie they'd shared throughout the evening started to fracture as they both stood, quiet and keeping their distance, in the shiny brass elevator. He studied their reflection, loving the way they looked.

Together.

"Sloan…" he said at the same instant she whispered his name.

"You go." She waved her hand, which clutched her purse in a death grip, at him.

"Right." A cheery bell dinged their arrival. Mark placed his palm on the small of her back to steer her from the elevator. "Here's the thing. I planned to drop you off at your door. Beg for one hell of a goodnight kiss. Maybe even fill my palms with your perfect ass and grind my rock-hard cock against your softness while we were at it. But now, I don't want to let go."

He turned her toward him then cupped her cheeks in his palm. "I don't want tonight to end."

Mark explored her parted lips, sipping from them but not ravaging before he resumed their march toward home. He left it to her to make the next move, to tell him if she craved him too.

Not one single word split the deafening silence as they approached Sloan's apartment. Twenty feet had never seemed so far. The anticipation almost killed him but he wouldn't push. If the same urgency driving him didn't consume her, he wouldn't pressure her because everything he'd said last night still held true.

A meaningless fuck didn't interest him.

The difference tonight was his acknowledgement of the fact sex with Sloan could never be casual or insignificant. Lynn had given him some advice earlier. It'd gone the same way for her. She'd known in the short hours she'd spent with Sebastian while their flights had been delayed he would be special to her. Forever. Even if things didn't work out long-term.

Their encounter marked a turning point in his life.

Hell, Mark would settle for going inside and sleeping. Holding Sloan through the night would be better than tossing and turning alone, dreaming of her until he rushed back to her door the moment his blaring alarm clock proclaimed the morning.

The jingle of her keys made him grit his teeth as he calculated the odds on whether she intended to let him in or leave him standing in the hallway, staring at the entrance to her apartment. She still hadn't uttered a single syllable by the time she turned the lock and cracked the door.

He gulped when she rested her forehead on the polished wood frame for the span of several heartbeats. Her shoulders shook beneath the force of her erratic breaths. The keys rattled softly in her trembling hand.

Then she pivoted, and the fire in her gorgeous eyes lit something inside him. "Come inside, Marco. I can't bear for the night to end here either."

"Yes." He couldn't express his emotions adequately in

English. The language he'd spoken since grade school evaporated from his mind. He murmured to her in Italian as he backed her into the room.

It felt like an erotic do-over as he gathered her into his arms for a drugging kiss. This is how things should have gone this morning. His heart rate raced.

They went from zero to sixty in no time flat, not bothering to stop mauling each other long enough to shut the door properly. He kicked it closed then kept their momentum going, banging into the desk, shifting a picture on the wall with his shoulder and knocking over a lamp as they stripped and made out simultaneously.

He couldn't bear to sacrifice a single point of contact.

The moment their bare skin met, chest to chest—or chest to abs more like it—he pressed closer to increase the amount of surface area touching to the max. But part of him mourned missing out on the view.

Mark forced himself to separate them. He bent his knees then scooped Sloan into his arms. Either she gave him the strength of two men or she was as light and slender as she looked. He could have carried her to the moon. But fortunately, the bed lay much closer than that.

He deposited her—as gently as he could manage despite the yearning raging inside him—before transferring his weight to the mattress, hovering over her on straight-locked arms. He imagined her, right here, the night before while she talked to him on the phone and played with herself until she came. For him.

Dio, the thought was spicy enough to give him a fever.

He sampled her swollen lips, devouring the taste of the wine they'd shared along with the flavor he now associated with her alone. The enthusiastic passion she returned would have knocked his socks off if he'd been wearing any. Intense, raw and urgent, her matching desire blew him away.

Then something occurred to him. If she read the same books as Lynn, she probably masturbated often, lying awake long into the night, filling the dim room with whimpers as she caressed herself to a fantasy. His abdomen clenched, making his cock bob against Sloan's pale, soft belly. The fluffy tufts of her trimmed pubic hair tickled his balls.

Could he last long enough to pull off the idea coalescing in his mind?

He hoped so because the devious plan had him hornier than he could ever remember being before, including the time he and Sebastian had taken home the entire cheerleading squad after one of their early events. Those gymnasts had been young, willing and undeniably limber.

Still, the memory of all those girls together had nothing on this moment—on the single, sophisticated woman stretching him to his limits. Something in him changed, shifting gears.

"Sloan?" He nibbled on her collarbone while he waited for his question to penetrate the fog of desire they created together.

"Hmm?" Her breathless response pumped his cock up more.

"Read to me."

"What?" She stopped scoring his shoulders with the light scratches proclaiming she couldn't get enough of his body to stare at him as though he'd lost his mind. If the passion inside her burned as hot as it did in him, he understood why. But he had an idea. A dirty, naughty, fabulous idea.

"What's your favorite book? Do you have it with you?"

"Yeah." She still seemed confused, but she'd catch on quick once he initialized his plan. "It's in my bag. Don't laugh but I take it everywhere."

"So it's in your briefcase?" He hopped from the bed, glad to see his agility hadn't gone the way of his patience, consumed by the promise of ecstasy to come. This night could surpass his high expectations. Because, for the first time, he shared it with someone who mattered. The closest he'd come to emotional connection before this had been the ménage he'd had with Sebastian and Lynn on the corporate jet, but that hadn't been about him. Not really.

He shook his head then asked her again. "The bag by your desk?"

"Yes."

He glanced over his shoulder at her and groaned. She propped herself on one elbow to watch as he riffled through the pockets. The pose made her look like something out of the Renaissance paintings he'd studied on class trips growing up. His love of the female form had been born then.

He wished he had a fraction of the Italian masters' talent so he could capture Sloan's magnificence for future generations to marvel over. The most beautiful woman alive deserved to be immortalized.

"This one?" He held up a well-used book. The cover featured a man and woman locked together beneath a waterfall.

"Mmm." Her eyes turned glassy as her imagination carried her to the places contained within the text.

Oh yeah, a *very* good idea.

He flipped through the pages on his return journey to their bed. The creases in the spine and the dog-eared corners clearly marked her favorite passages. But when he rested the book in his palm, it fell open to the same spot every time.

Bingo.

Mark stole a glimpse of the chapter, scanning the explicit text. This would work perfectly. He switched the bedside lamp on low then handed her the book.

"Read it aloud." He shook the novel in her direction, pages fluttering, until she wrapped her fingers around the paper. "Start from here."

He pointed to the paragraph he'd noticed.

"I-I can't." Was Sloan really blushing?

"Really?" He grinned. "You've read this thing more than once—"

"About a hundred times."

"But you can't say the words? That's adorable." He trailed his fingers along the tops of her breasts, up her neck and to her flaming cheeks. "What kind of Cougar are you? Come on, Sloan. Read it to me."

"Now?" She whimpered. "Don't tease me, Marco. Give me what I need. Or let me take it. I'll show you exactly what kind of Cougar I am."

"Tempting. But no. Read." He straddled her calves then took his plump cock in hand. A groan burst from his chest when she watched him stroke the aching flesh. Nothing meek about her stare. "I'll take care of you."

She lunged forward, bending over. Her tongue slipped between her full lips and swiped the bead of moisture from the head of his cock. His eyes rolled in his skull. It took every shred of control he possessed to keep from thrusting into her alluring mouth, exactly as she must have planned.

Sloan's shoulders filled his palms as he restrained her then abandoned his post. He collapsed onto his back on the fluffy comforter. "It's not polite to talk with your mouth full."

"Holy shit. Either you are the most stubborn man on earth or I've forgotten how to do that right."

"I believe you're capable of a blowjob for the history books, but you can practice later if it makes you happy."

"If you're concerned with what pleases *me,* then you'll quit screwing around and start fucking me instead."

He grinned when she rose above him, the erotic romance clasped in her shaking fingers.

"There you go. Say the words and I'll make them come true. Neither of us has to suffer like this any longer."

Sloan shot him a look brimming with gratitude and relief. It almost broke his heart—and his resolve—but, before he could reach for her, she cleared her throat and began to read. If she'd recited the alphabet, her husky rasp still would have inflated his cock, but the sensual content of her speech made his balls tense as they gathered tight to his body in response.

"*Nicholas had frustrated Simone until all rational thought fled. She reacted on instinct, shoving him backward onto the bed then pouncing onto his supine form. 'If you want to run your mouth, put it to better use than arguing with me.'*"

Sloan surprised Mark. She planted one palm on his sternum then threw her leg over his torso, pinning him to the bed. The heat of her pussy singed his chest, leaving a glistening trail of arousal to mark him as her property when she settled lower.

Looked as if she took this Cougar business serious.

Fuck, yes.

"*Nicholas didn't object. Instead he cupped his hands around her thighs then slid them upward until his long fingers wrapped around the curve of her hips. His diabolical grin proved he'd antagonized her on purpose. He loved to fire her up then cool her down. The tender grasp of his broad hands guaranteed he'd never hurt her, no matter their petty disagreements. He supported her while granting her the freedom to use him as she wished, knowing they'd both reap the rewards.*"

Mark groaned when his fingers encountered the soft skin of Sloan's perfect form. He mimicked the hero's actions, caressing her with stokes sure enough to impress but malleable enough to adapt to her direction. A hitch in Sloan's voice rewarded his effort. His nostrils flared as the scent of her arousal reached him.

Despite her initial objections, lubrication saturated her pussy as she turned the page. Strands of the viscous fluid spanned the tiny gap between her puffy lips and his heaving abdomen, like threads in an erotic spider web, when her juices overflowed.

The sight caused him to salivate.

"*'I'm sorry, sweetheart. I didn't mean for things to get out of hand. I shouldn't have yelled like that. But, Jesus, you're sexy when you argue.' The breath forming Nicholas' apology buffeted her over-sensitized flesh. 'Let me make it up to you.'*

"His fingertips dug into the crevice between her ass cheeks when he squeezed, pulling her closer to his parted lips. The stiff set of Simone's anger-flushed shoulders relaxed as he seduced her. She arched her spine, thrusting her breasts forward into her waiting palms. The nipples hardened as she kneaded the soft flesh."

"Beautiful." Mark sighed as he watched Sloan blossom above him. She plucked at one nipple with her free hand. The gentle pinch caused a visible ripple of her svelte stomach muscles, squeezing another drop of honey from her channel and onto his pecs. He reached up to assist but laughed when she slapped his hand away, keeping true to the text, without tearing her gaze from the pages of her book.

Dio, she turned him on with every move.

Sloan reached down and covered his lips with two fingers. He kissed them to atone for breaking his character, though he swore the hero of the novel would have said something similar if he'd had the chance.

Engrossed in the story, Sloan read on. In all the years he'd studied her from afar, he never would have guessed she'd be so kinky in bed. A pleasant surprise. He loved every facet of her adventurousness. He'd have to brainstorm lots of creative ideas to keep her entertained. Later. Much later.

"Nicholas groaned then urged Simone to scoot up. It was as if he didn't taste her soon, he'd die. She absorbed his longing, the

radiance of his desire for her making her glow. Despite their tiff, nothing could erase the magic they generated together. Her anxiety faded, replaced with relief and the peace she found in his arms."

Mark gulped. He could relate. He dragged Sloan higher on his body, aligning her pussy with his mouth. Praying she didn't waste any time continuing. He couldn't stand to wait one more minute to prove they had the potential to be legendary.

"Granting Nicholas a reprieve, Simone sank onto his face. She ground her aching pussy against the flexed muscle of his protruding tongue, the soft ridges of his opened lips and the firm swell of his now-soaked chin.

"He could be infuriating but he always made up for it somehow.

"Simone rode Nicholas' talented mouth as he attempted to ingest every ounce of her pleasure. Her earlier aggravation dissolved as she accepted his apology and opened herself, eradicating the barrier their anger had caused. When they came together like this, nothing else mattered. She rubbed her clit against his nose while he rimmed the contours of her slit with the tip of his tongue in the exact pattern she liked best. He'd tested her mercilessly until he'd uncovered all her secrets."

If Mark had known stories could be this good, he'd actually have read a few books instead of faking his way through school reports. No wonder Lynn had Sebastian looking completely relaxed and sated after she finished a novel or, shit, even a single chapter.

Mark had lost count of the number of times he'd had to cover while his friends sneaked into a crew trailer or a bathroom or a supply closet on the race circuit after Lynn spent the afternoon entertaining herself while he and Bastian took practice runs.

This time he wanted to show Sloan she didn't have to enjoy this alone. She could take charge of her destiny, of her pleasure. For them both.

He growled against the ultrasoft flesh of her pussy as he followed her script. His tongue lapped at the scrumptious juice flowing from her core. She responded, rocking until she wrung pleasure from each contour of his face.

The sheer delight in her tone as she continued her story in a somewhat ragged voice thrilled him. Wild, wanton and sweet, she stole his breath.

"*Simone's head thrashed from side to side, knocking loose the clip holding her hair. A riot of curls tumbled down her back, dusting her shoulders with each toss of her head. She leaned back, bracing herself on her lover's taut abdomen as he continued to turn her ire to excitement. He could inspire so many violent emotions in her. Their bond filled her with awe.*"

Mark peered between Sloan's full breasts to watch her fling her mane of thick, rich locks across her sensitive skin. Her nails dug into his stomach and her knees squeezed his shoulders when he hummed his approval against her pussy.

"*The attentive licks, nips and sucks of Nicholas' mouth communicated his caring more clearly than if he'd written her a beautiful sonnet. He knew how to touch her to amplify her pleasure and he did so. Repeatedly. His devotion melted her restraint. Before she knew what happened, the initial stirrings of her orgasm fluttered deep in her belly.*"

Sloan cried out above him when he drew the hard knot of her clit between his lips, laving the tender nerves with a fraction of the wonder and respect she inspired in him. He burrowed into her soaked flesh, prodding her to continue if she could.

If not, he'd use his imagination to lead her the rest of the way. He couldn't wait to observe her ecstasy. Knowing he pleased her filled a void in his soul he hadn't known existed. He longed to transform into whatever she liked, whatever she needed, suspecting she would gladly do the same for him.

"*Nicholas sensed Simone nearing the brink. He slid one hand from her thigh to tease the contracting edge of her opening. The prodding of his blunt digit made her jerk, slathering his cheek with more of her wetness. He groaned his appreciation then pressed harder, sinking his finger in her body as far as he could reach.*"

Mark took it as a good sign when Sloan dropped her book. His finger penetrated the tight mouth of her pussy. Her channel clung to him, hugging him, smothering him with her heat.

Still, she searched blindly with her free hand to reclaim the novel and her place. It took her a ludicrous number of tries to continue, her sentences choppy and breathless.

"When Nicholas had buried two thick fingers in her, Simone held on by a thread. She didn't want to surrender so soon. Not when it meant an end to the bliss drowning her. He paused to murmur against her soaked pussy. 'Let go, Simone. I have you. Always.'

"Despite her resistance, Simone lost the fight against her torrential need when Nicholas scissored his fingers inside her pussy. She came around them as he curled the digits, pressing the rough patch of her G-spot against her pubic bone—"

Sloan screamed her orgasm loud enough Sebastian and Lynn had to have heard it down the hall. At least they would know he'd done a good job of pleasing his gorgeous Cougar. A ferocious surge of pride washed over him for matching her fantasy. The compatibility of their dreams tasted nearly as good as the wetness flooding Sloan's pussy, coating his tongue.

Mark continued to lap her swollen tissue, stroking through the spasms of her ringed muscles with his embedded fingers. His free hand snaked up her side to cup her breast, extending the waves of her climax. His hips arched from the bed as the need to fuck her overwhelmed his logic.

When she went limp, he altered his grip, supporting her shoulders and neck as he guided her to sprawl on her side next to him. He reached for the shirt he'd discarded somewhere nearby to wipe his face before kissing her, but she tangled her fingers in his hair and dragged him to her before he could perform the courtesy most of his lovers had demanded.

Seemed she didn't mind messy—another turn-on for him. Nothing about her struck him as artificial. She didn't hide her desire or act as if the remnants of her ecstasy disgusted her after she'd found relief.

He should have quit fucking shallow fangirls years ago.

Their endless tangle of tongues, locking of lips and exchange of pleasure resurrected his passion, stronger after witnessing her pure lust. He grabbed his hard-on, content to solve his own problem as she lounged in a sensual daze. But Sloan would have none of that.

She reached between them, purring when she knocked his hand aside to fist his cock. "I think it's your turn to read, lover boy."

Her devious smirk told him the scene hadn't finished there.

Holy shit.

"You're up for more?" He didn't want her to continue for his sake alone if she was sated. It wasn't as though he expected payback for satisfying her.

"I'm just getting started. I have a ton of time to make up for. Play with me, Marco."

She laughed when he scrambled for the book, rummaging beneath the crumpled covers until he unearthed the slightly bent volume. He flipped past the section they'd already reenacted. His eyes bugged out when he saw there were two more pages before the next chapter break.

Two whole pages of scorching sex. He didn't think he could last that long.

When Sloan winked then turned over, getting to her hands and knees, he didn't have a choice. He had to fuck her no matter what the story held. Resisting her near-perfect ass sticking into the air would prove impossible.

Mark heaved a sigh of relief when he read the next segment.

"Nicholas petted his lover's flank when she presented herself for his use. All their earlier tension erased in the wake of their sharing. He knelt between her spread knees, nudging them farther apart until she relied on his grip to keep her relaxed frame steady. He would never let her fall."

Out of options, Mark set the book on Sloan's back, supporting her with one hand while the other pinned the pages open.

"Nicholas ground his straining cock against Simone's rounded cheeks, nestling the engorged length into the valley of her ass. With two fingers, he aimed the tip toward her pretty pink pussy, still clenching periodically with the aftershocks of her first orgasm."

Mark hated to shatter the illusion they spun but his conscience forced him to return to reality long enough to ask, "Are you on the Pill?"

"Yes. And I'm clean. I've been tested every six months since my husband cheated on me." Sloan peaked over her shoulder as though afraid of his reaction. An insane urge to pummel her ex evaporated when he realized she waited with unspoken questions in her eyes. He nodded in response.

"Me too," he groaned. "Never fucked without a condom before but…it's not here, not a part of our story."

"Nicholas and Simone would never permit a barrier between them. Nothing between us either." She rocked toward his waiting hard-on, notching the tip in her opening, causing them both to groan at the contact.

"No, nothing."

"*Nicholas leaned forward, introducing his thick shaft to Simone an inch at a time. No matter how often they made love, her resilient body stretched to accommodate him when he entered her as though they'd never done it before, as though they were made for each other. Because they were.*"

A perfect fit.

"Yes!" Mark shouted as he inched deeper within Sloan until his balls came to rest against the moist skin of her body. He took several heartbeats to absorb the importance of the moment—to savor the first time they fused together—though it seemed more like a homecoming than an expedition. She covered him like a glove. Snug. Warm. Comforting.

"*Nicholas paused to gather the shreds of his control, dedicated to ensuring Simone's satisfaction. His hands roamed the landscape of her body from her shoulders, along her back, to her ass then around to her front to cup her breasts where they hung heavy beneath her petite frame. When the churning desire in his balls settled to a manageable roar, he began to fuck. His ass flexed as he thrust and retreated, reveling in the damp heat caressing his stiff cock. He wished he could get closer even than this, to reveal his soul so she could see for herself the reverence she propagated.*

"*He couldn't decide what felt better, the first touch of her sultry flesh on the ultrasensitive head of his dick or the storm of satisfaction engulfing his entire shaft when he bottomed out, just before he withdrew to start another cycle. No matter how many times he repeated the motion, both seemed like unsurpassable delights.*"

Mark grunted his agreement. Sloan's pussy enticed him to fuck harder, faster as he made his own comparison. Balls-deep, he decided. It had to be best when he was buried to the hilt in her luscious body and they connected as completely as possible.

"Before long, Nicholas couldn't prevent himself from slamming into the receptacle of Simone's body. She braced herself on the headboard, absorbing his thrusts, begging for more by arching her spine and loving him back.

"He gave her what she wanted, what they needed. He fucked her hard. Rough. Frantic. Until nothing mattered but joining them more with each stroke."

At this point, Mark read for his own benefit. Sloan knew the story by heart and acted her part before he squawked the descriptions out. It became difficult to talk, to pronounce the steamy lines in between his pants and groans, his indulgence in Sloan's ideal body.

He flipped the page of the book resting in the small of her back, holding it in place with one hand. With his other palm, he anchored her waist as he hammered into her greedy pussy.

The intoxicating friction generated by her rhythmic squeezes and his impaling cock had him seeing stars. Still, something didn't feel quite right. He didn't want to come like this. He slowed to read another paragraph, only now realizing he'd stopped his oration several minutes ago, lured into silence by the perfection of their passion.

"But right when Nicholas felt himself about to spiral out of control, he tore his erection from the embrace of his lover's channel and nudged her to her back."

Mark propped the novel against the headboard while he covered Sloan with his body, blanketing her smaller form. The complete connection blanked his mind, leaving him helpless to do anything but savor the contact. Then he gritted his teeth and cleared his throat.

"'Why...did...you stop?' Simone panted as she gathered Nicholas close, surrounding him in the shelter of her embrace, pillowing him on the softness of her welcoming body. The concern shadowing her face guaranteed their earlier quarrel had been all but forgotten.

"'I want to look into your eyes when we come together. I need to know that hasn't changed. Never will. We can figure anything else out. Together.' He rested his forehead on hers then glided home. Her arms wound around him, holding him next to

her breast. Her heartbeat pounded in time with his. Nothing could match this. When they coupled, nothing else mattered. He thanked the stars for giving him the woman of his dreams.

"Not just once but every night of their lives."

Mark couldn't imagine getting so lucky. He'd settle for this moment.

This one utterly pristine moment.

"'It didn't take long before Simone granted his wish. They stared, unblinking, as they let go together. Their orgasms struck simultaneously. Warm blasts of Nicholas' cum shot from his cock, echoed by her soft cries. Spasms racked her body, drawing several additional jets from his tense balls in an endless cycle of euphoric release."

Mark mirrored the lucky bastard. His gaze locked with Sloan's as he surrendered. He rocked inside her, feeding her every last drop of his come as she continued to milk him. Gentle moans and sighs accompanied each contraction of her pussy around his softening cock until, finally, he rested inside her, unwilling to abandon her embrace.

How long they stayed that way he couldn't say, but it might have been the most amazing time of his life.

When Mark stirred, Sloan's fingers tangled in his hair. She soothed him with tender touches until he was fairly certain he would survive the barrage of rapture and the near explosion of his heart she had instigated.

The sting in his eyes horrified him. Straining to read while fucking must have dried them out—a bedroom hazard he'd never expected.

He swiped at the hint of moisture at the corners surreptitiously as he rolled, taking Sloan with him so he reclined on his back and she lay on his chest, truly looking like a cat who'd slurped an entire bowl of cream and then some. The bright red of her nails on his tan skin shot a twinge through his exhausted cock.

They breathed together, sharing the consummation of their joining for long minutes until he couldn't help but speculate. "Can I ask you something?"

"Uh-huh."

Mark traced the edges of Sloan's satisfied smile with one

finger then wondered aloud, "Of all the books you've read, what makes that one your favorite? Why is that scene so special?"

She bit her lip and closed her eyes.

"No, Sloan." He shook her gently until she reopened them, surprising him as always with the gorgeous depths of her hazel eyes. "Don't do that. Please. Not after what we shared. Stay my aggressive, sexy, Cougar."

"Sorry." She winced. "The physical part is easier. I don't have a lot of practice with this kind of…intimacy."

"Me either, but let's try it. Say whatever you want. I can take it and you might like sharing."

More like confiding, but he didn't want to scare her.

She nodded then shot him a feral grin. "Well, the sex is tame compared to some of the books I read, that's true."

Mark groaned. *That* was tame? What if he'd picked a different book? Or a different chapter?

"But something about this one feels… real. The connection between the characters gets me every time. They aren't flawless. They screw stuff up. But they always come back to each other. To the undying passion between them. I cry during their fights, laugh when they're happy and get turned-on when they have sex." She sighed then nodded as if to herself. "Their story is everything I wanted for myself and gave up on when I couldn't repair things with my husband. A relationship that's not always utopian, but where the love—affection and friendship—endures."

"You deserve that, Sloan." Mark despised the shadows in her eyes but couldn't bear to ruin their calm by pushing her further. Not tonight.

He smiled as he tucked a strand of hair behind her ear. "All that and more."

Then he kissed her, snuggled her close to his heart and drifted off to sleep.

Chapter Five

Sloan watched out the window as streaks of emerald foliage gave way to industrial buildings. One of the other crew members had taken them to Guangzhou to catch the high-speed train to Hong Kong. The drive to the station bombarded her with sights and experiences. Every time she left international housing and immersed herself in the environment around her, reality annihilated her preconceived notions.

China, to her, consisted of so many contrasts. The terrain, the cultures and the fascinating mix of contemporary and ancient all jumbled together to create a diverse and captivating land. If she spent ten years here, she'd never absorb all the nuances. Asian aesthetics—buildings with tile roofs, paper lanterns and bold red slashes—surrounded her with beauty even in crowded, rundown neighborhoods.

She'd never been somewhere she felt more isolated—a complete foreigner—and yet reassured that many human truths were universal. A smile from a child in a stroller, graffiti in the form of characters etched into the broad leaves of tropical plants, a passerby waving hello, hawkers shouting from overcrowded stalls, and taxis blowing their horns were familiar but different.

Guangzhou appealed to her. It teemed with industrious people going about their day-to-day life, embracing a simplicity that highlighted how many times Americans overcomplicated things. Here, an object didn't have to have a name brand stamped on the side to get the job done.

A man on a bicycle delivered supplies to the market in polystyrene boxes piled high enough to transport nearly as much as a U-Haul back in the States. A woman bore a stick across her shoulders from which two baskets of laundry swinged. Scaffolding, made entirely of bamboo, teemed with construction workers who wore no safety gear, not even boots. Their rustic sandals slapping on bare feet as they scaled the hastily erected structure highlighted real differences from the world she belonged to and forced her to consider the luxuries she took for granted.

Still, the lack of precautions designed with the lowest common denominator in mind made her realize how sterile her existence in the US had been at times. She wouldn't trade her heritage or her country for any other, but gaining perspective couldn't hurt either.

Not all things were strange. Modern men and women in suits trudged off to a work day similar to the ones she'd suffered through when she clocked time in an office. But the smell of street-meat carts and fruit on a stick made the mundane seem exotic.

"Would you like to try some?" Mark caught her checking out the red kebab of candied fruit as they exited their friend's car at the station. It looked like something she'd find at a carnival back home.

"What is it?" she asked Mark, but he shrugged then looked toward Lynn for assistance.

"It's called *tanghulu*." Lynn swerved toward the vendor, dragging Sebastian with her. "It's delectable. Sweet and filling for breakfast. The apple-looking things are hawthorn fruit. Some of the vendors use other ingredients too."

"This one looks like it has kiwi and sesame seeds sprinkled on top of the clear glaze." Sloan inspected the offerings with a smile and a nod at the man working the cart.

Mark moaned. "Damn, this smells great. I'm getting one to hold me over for the ride. Anyone else?"

In the end, they each tried a different variety. The vendor seemed disappointed when they refused to haggle over the price but, despite the downturn in the economy, enough food to feed four adults cost six Yuan—less than a single American dollar.

It didn't seem right to pay less than that.

It truly was a treat for her taste buds.

Not to mention, watching the men eat the sticky snacks from the foot-and-a-half-long skewer had naughty ideas flashing through her mind. What was wrong with her that spending the night with Mark hadn't quenched her cravings?

Bold and daring, she'd woken during the early morning and taken advantage of her lover's steely erection prodding her backside. When he roused again several hours later, he'd repaid the favor with a smooth, sensual fuck that enticed her to relax and allow pleasure to consume her.

"*Amico*, swap a bite. I want to try yours." Sebastian held his skewer toward Mark, who leaned forward and ripped a hunk of fleshy fruit from the rod with his teeth. He groaned as a spurt of liquid oozed from the treat.

"Damn, that's awesome." Mark returned the favor, extending his stick to Sebastian. "Why don't we have these things at home? I could get used to this."

Sebastian bit into one of the last morsels, his lips nearly brushing the side of Mark's hand. His throat worked as he swallowed the offering then licked his lips. "Too bad we don't have time for another round. These rocked."

Sloan's eyes nearly bugged out of her head at the exchange. Did they even realize how hot they were together? Mark had said they'd shared intimate situations before. She believed it after seeing how natural and at ease they were around each other.

When she turned, she saw Lynn staring as she fanned herself. The day hadn't built enough swelter for that until the two guys started eating from each other's hands. At least she hadn't been the only one to notice. If the desire etched on her new friend's face was any indication, Lynn had enjoyed witnessing the exchange as much as she did.

Sloan had to look away before she spontaneously combusted. She studied the pattern of stones beneath her shoes until her breathing returned to normal. Then her gaze lifted to Mark's to find him grinning as he licked the last of the juicy sweetness from his fingers with extra relish, promising he knew where her mind had gone—straight into the gutter.

Desire crackled in the air between them.

Lynn broke the moment when she laughed out loud. "You two are great together, you know that? You don't even have to be touching and I can see the attraction."

"Pretty awesome, isn't it?" Mark winked at them both.

"Yes, it definitely is." Sloan grinned. "Careful though, or Lynn might get the wrong idea. Unless of course, you want her and Sebastian to see how well you can clean that stick off."

Mark froze.

For one horrible second she feared she'd taken their playful banter too far. Then the dilation of his pupils along with his gruff tone convinced Sloan her instincts had been dead-on. He'd hoped to tease all *three* of them, not her alone.

It'd worked. And she found she liked the idea.

"We better head to the platform or we'll miss the next train." Sebastian cleared his throat then scrubbed his hands over his face, the bulge in his jeans impossible to miss. Lynn dropped a chaste peck on Mark's cheek then took her fiancé's arm, letting the subject drop with no hard feelings.

They hustled into the station, cleared customs then boarded a sleek, advanced train. Public transportation here exceeded all options available at home. Sloan wished she could hop on something like this in NYC and zip over to the Midwest—quick, cheap and green.

Quiet and introspective, Mark ushered her into the window seat in a row for two passengers while Sebastian and Lynn took the pair of spaces across the aisle from them in the remarkably comfortable car. When Sloan peeked over at the other couple, they were making out, indulging in a long, slow mating of lips and tongues.

Despite Sebastian's attempt to battle his urges, it seemed Mark had inspired a sexual reaction in his partner.

She grinned at the couple, nudging Mark in the ribs with her elbow. He blinked then shifted his stare from the seatback in front of him. Had Sebastian's earlier refusal to play their game upset him?

Sloan squeezed his hand. The young man looked into her eyes, allowing her to study him closely. Slight lines had formed at the corners of his mouth. "Are you okay?"

"Terrific." He beamed. "I'm on an adventure with my Cougar and my two best friends after an amazing night. What more could I want?"

The wistful cast to his rhetorical question made her itch to fill whatever void plagued him. She folded their armrest up then tugged his hand until he abolished the gap between them.

When she settled against his warm side, something hard jabbed her hip. "What do you have in your pocket? Or are you happy to sit next to me?"

She wiggled her eyebrows and he laughed, shaking free from the gloom shrouding him.

"Sorry to disappoint. That's my iPod." He shifted to one side, delving into the ripped, European-style denim hugging his slim hips for the device. "I like to listen to music when I travel."

"Who do you have queued up?" She wrapped her fingers around his wrist, loving the contrast of her crimson nails and his olive complexion. When he rotated the screen, she frowned. "Angels and Airwaves. Huh. Never heard of them. Damn, that makes me feel old."

"Why should it? Here, we'll listen together. Then you'll know they kick ass." He handed her one of his earbuds before situating the other so he could hear too. "This album is my favorite. It's called *Love*."

Sloan's chest lurched at the look he shared with her—hot enough she wondered why she hadn't melted into a puddle on the floor. She sighed then rested her head on his chest, canted so she could watch the scenery fly by.

The music had a hypnotic quality to it. Long sections of rhythmic electronic echoes left her plenty of time to reflect on the bond growing between her and Mark. Not to mention the link they shared with the other couple on their journey. Then the music picked up, turning into a sexy rock song. She wished they were in a club, the music blaring so she could dance with Mark to the soulful melodies.

"This is great."

Mark nodded, singing along softly. It felt as though he'd written the beautiful lyrics for her. By sharing, exposing himself further, he tempted her to drop her inhibitions.

She shifted in her seat, the motion rubbing her breast against his ribs. He reciprocated, grooving in time to the beat with subtle motions that pressed them together. His fingers tapped a complex syncopation on her knee as they swayed along with the song.

By the time the music ended, she would have given a month's salary for some privacy. She had an insane urge to take care of Mark, to ease the dissatisfaction she sensed in his soul. Something about his tirade the other morning, and the way he reacted to Sebastian's subtle rebuke at the station, made her suspect he considered himself second string in the men's friendship.

The fury he'd lashed out with had stemmed from hurt.

Everyone notices Sebastian, not me. I'm just the navigator. Some loser who rides along with a superstar and drools over smoking-hot, professional ladies who are completely out of my league unless they decide to slum it with some young, dumb, walking hard-on for a night of endless fucking.

Not that she got any such vibe from Sebastian. Hell, the driver would probably be horrified if he knew what Mark thought. She tensed as she considered the years Mark might have suffered in silence under the guise of friendship.

Of course, her lover chose then to focus on her line of sight. When he saw her looking at Sebastian, he stiffened and withdrew.

"Come back, Marco," she whispered. "It's not what you think."

"Women have always preferred him. You don't have to hide it. I'm used to it." He impressed her because he really meant it. How many times had he sacrificed what he wanted for Sebastian? His generosity enhanced his appeal, though he'd taken it to unhealthy levels. "But I have to warn you, he's committed to Lynn."

Maybe she could help Mark see the pattern of self-destructive behavior ensnaring him. She didn't intend to preach to him but she could try to demonstrate how much more he was than a stud for hire.

Sexy, loyal, generous, funny and gentle but fierce when cornered, he deserved better than believing himself second best. Their time together would be sweeter if she knew he'd have a shot at sustained happiness after their affair ended—because, surely, once she restored his confidence, he'd ditch her faster than their world-record lap time.

Some lucky woman would be thrilled to have him. The bitch.

"Well, *this* woman wants you. For you. Not as a way to get closer to your friend." Sloan captured his unsteady hand and guided it to her thigh, beneath the hem of her flouncy skirt. After a quick look around to ensure no one else had come near, she encouraged him to seek out the source of the wetness dampening her thighs.

She revealed her surprise.

"*Dio*," he panted. "No panties? You're soaked."

"All for you. Because of you." She kissed the side of his neck, over the spot she'd identified as one of his pleasure points. When she'd nipped him there this morning, he'd emptied himself inside her with a roar.

Sloan whimpered at the memory.

"Spread your legs, Cougar. Let me give you pleasure."

"No."

His head jerked backward until he could meet her stare. Confusion swirled in his warm brown eyes. "Because we're in public?"

"No, you drive me crazy no matter where we are." Sloan checked the empty car one last time before making up her mind. "Because *I* want to service *you*. Right here, right now."

"That's not a good idea…"

"I don't care." Before he could object, she shoved his faded t-shirt up his abdomen, tucked her fingertips into his waistband and ripped open his fly. She purred when she caught sight of his bare cock standing at attention.

Very ready despite his protests.

Sloan scooted to the edge of her seat then bent to bury her face in his lap. She licked him from root to tip, measuring his long hard-on with her tongue. She paused to glance up at him from her perch and whisper, "But if I get thrown in a Chinese prison for giving you the greatest blowjob of all time, make sure you don't leave me there to rot. Stripes aren't my thing."

Lost in each other, they both jumped when Sebastian laughed at her joke.

"Oops. Don't mind me and Lynn." Sebastian grinned when Sloan blushed. "I've got your back, Mark. Enjoy. It's not every day you get an offer like that. Besides, you know how Lynn gets off on watching."

A surge of excitement surprised Sloan. She wouldn't have said she had a single exhibitionist tendency before today, but suddenly—here, now, with these people—she wanted nothing more than to demonstrate how Mark improved her.

He transformed her from a jilted, middle-aged divorcee to a fearless, feral Cougar on the prowl without trying.

She dragged the cascade of her hair across his satiny flesh, pleased when he hissed and clenched his hand on his thigh as though afraid he'd rocket from his place. With her head angled, she opened her eyes and gauged the reaction of their audience of two.

Sebastian had pivoted so his shoulders rested against the window and one leg propped on the seats while the other braced both his and Lynn's weight on the floor. He held his fiancé on his lap, fondling her breasts through her clothes as he ground his cock against her ass.

Not a single shred of anxiety or awkwardness plagued Sloan when she caught the naked admiration in their gazes. Satisfied, she faced Mark one more time. "You want me to suck you? Right here, where anyone could see? Where your friends *will* see?"

"Fuck yes. Sloan," he panted. "Put your mouth on me. Please."

CHAPTER SIX

Mark gaped at the gorgeous woman lingering near his cock. He couldn't believe he'd asked her to suck him. Fucking begged like a starving man in front of his closest friends. He didn't give a rat's ass. If Sloan didn't touch him in the next five seconds, he would die.

Her knuckles grazed his hard-on when she widened the gap of his fly, causing his pelvis to jerk reflexively. His abdomen flexed at the first contact of her supple skin. Sloan grinned then wrapped her dainty fingers around the base of his erection.

"Hurry, before someone comes," he urged her as he angled his hips to give her optimal access.

"I *hope* someone comes." Lynn teased from across the aisle. In his peripheral vision, Mark saw her hand disappear below her skirt, drawing a muffled curse from Sebastian. "The more the merrier."

"I love it when you get dirty, *tesoro*." Sebastian's appreciative growl inspired Mark.

"Do it, Sloan. Let me show them how hot you make me." He reclined farther into the cushion of the seat, granting her room to work. "This won't take long. I've wanted you again since the moment I left your tight pussy this morning."

Her green eyes sparkled a moment before she attacked him. She opened her bright red lips and inhaled his cock, leaving scarlet stains as she glided along his shaft.

He could only moan and allow her to have her way with him, powerless to do more than relish her attention. When her lips wrapped around the base of his cock, she swallowed, caressing his blunt head with the muscles of her throat. Her tongue darted out to swipe over the wrinkled skin of his scrotum.

Five seconds after she'd started, Mark had to bang his skull on the headrest to keep from erupting all over her talented tongue. He never would have guessed being watched would rev his engine. She moved her hands to cover his wrists at his side, turning him on further. Knowing his friends observed such a remarkable woman servicing him filled him with pride.

Mark struggled to hang on when every swipe of her lips, bob of her head and suck of her mouth encouraged him to freefall. He lost track of the steady sway of the train car, the sounds of Lynn pleasuring herself and anything other than the woman devouring him.

His focus narrowed until she became the only thing in his universe. He pumped his hips, assisting her when she couldn't quite reach the last fraction of an inch of his cock. Desire roiled in his balls, eager to be unleashed.

Each second he endured her torture, he lost more control. She added a hand, strangling the base of his dick as she concentrated on the sensitive head.

"Oh fuck." He grunted. "Yes. More. There."

His fingers splayed, out of his command, straight and spread. Shivers racked his body. One more pass of her talented tongue and he'd be over the edge.

An annoying noise almost distracted him from the bliss raining around him but he ignored the disturbance and concentrated on the pleasure Sloan gave him.

Until the sound recurred.

"Sloan!" Sebastian hissed from across the aisle way. "Get up. Someone's coming. Move. Now!"

The thought of a stranger catching them in the act was more than Mark could bear. He tried to stop the tidal wave of rapture but he couldn't. As Sloan pulled off his cock, semen gushed from his balls.

The first crest of his orgasm hit, contracting every muscle in his body. In slow motion, he watched Sloan's eyes grow wide.

She reacted with feline instincts as he sat, helpless, in the throes of one of the most powerful climaxes of his life.

She grabbed his cock, taking the first spurt of milky fluid across her hand as she straddled his thighs, her skirt draping over their laps. The second must have decorated the soft hair on her pussy as she guided him to her core. By the third, she sank onto his straining shaft, welcoming him home.

Sloan bit his neck, probably to prevent a scream because, before he'd penetrated balls-deep, she went stiff in his arms. Her channel spasmed around him, squeezing several more blasts of come from his cock.

Mark clung to her, slamming his eyes shut, burying his face in her hair.

Somewhere far away, he heard Lynn cooking up a lame excuse for their behavior in broken English. It sounded as if she'd said they were upset, that he was comforting Sloan after bad news, but he couldn't manage to care. Come still oozed from the head of his cock, embedded deep in his lover's body.

Sloan trembled in his grip, her nails digging into his shoulders.

They stayed locked together, quiet, until Sebastian broke the silence. "He's gone."

Sloan sat up straight, putting a gap between their chests. He wished she hadn't moved. He missed her heat and her softness over his heart.

"Sorry about that. Bad timing." She kissed him sweetly.

His mind spun so much that he let her distract him for close to a minute before correcting her. "Perfect timing. *Dio*! Shooting deep into your pussy..."

He ended on a groan as an aftershock shook him.

"I almost didn't make it in time." She held up her palm for him to see. An opaque slash marked her pink skin. He leaned forward, intending to lick her clean when Lynn spoke up.

"Wait!" She panted. "He's inside you right now?"

"Yes." They both moaned together.

"Holy shit," Sebastian muttered reverently.

"Don't move," Lynn suggested. "Enjoy it. Let me see your hand, Sloan."

Mark looked to his lover with one eyebrow raised. Would she

do it?

Sloan nodded. “I’m going to give it to her.”

The two women together packed a punch.

Sebastian groaned, drawing his attention. “What did we do to get so lucky, a*mico*?”

“I don’t know.” Mark stroked Sloan’s hair, in awe of her. He gripped her wrist then extended it toward Lynn, who looked close to coming herself. Flushed cheeks, chest rising and falling rapidly, eyelids half-closed, she’d enjoyed their show.

When Sloan’s fingers hovered below Lynn’s face, his best friend’s woman dipped her head and licked the line of come from start to finish until she’d gathered all the opalescent fluid onto her tongue.

Sloan’s pussy clamped around Mark as her orgasm extended, wringing another wave of pleasure from him. He expected Lynn to swallow the sample but instead she turned to her fiancé.

“Taste them,” she whispered before she sealed their lips in a kiss.

The moment Sebastian indulged in the delicacy, sucking his fiancé’s tongue into his mouth, Lynn exploded. She released a series of escalating moans that Sloan echoed.

Mark hugged his partner closer, supporting her through another round of ecstasy. Her pussy squeezed his softening cock so hard it slipped from her grip. They both groaned at the loss.

Sebastian’s eyes darted from Lynn to Mark to Sloan and back in an endless loop. He cursed in Italian then grunted as his orgasm struck. He humped Lynn’s covered ass while he emptied his balls in his shorts, inspiring a sigh from both women.

Mark had seen Bastian come hundreds of times before when they’d shared women, or jacked off to porn during late nights on the circuit. Something about this time was different.

Yeah, he’s never had your sperm in his mouth when he shot before.

He wondered if Sloan noticed his cock twitch against her thigh.

The secret smile spreading against his neck, where her face rested in the crook of his shoulder, proved she had. Too exhausted to deal with the fallout of their spontaneous, reckless behavior, he closed his eyes, snuggled Sloan close then drifted off for the remainder of the ride.

The day had hardly begun but he couldn't image it ending much better than this.

* * * * *

Sloan shifted out of Mark's hold when his light snores caused her smile. How could he be such a stallion and so adorable at the same time?

She retrieved her laptop from her bag and flipped it open. Trains here supplied free wireless internet connectivity. She could definitely grow accustomed to this.

When her browser popped open, a chain of new blog posts clogged the screen. A giggle escaped her chest, disturbing Mark a bit. He snuffled then adjusted his position to lean closer to her before returning to a regular pattern of deep breathing.

Sloan petted his thick hair then returned her attention to the *Tempt the Cougar* blog.

Lynn: Good morning, Cougars! I'm writing while hurtling across Asia on a bullet train with the man of my dreams. Ah, I live a tough life. All kidding aside, I'm really excited. Sebastian and I are headed to check out Cheung Chau island near Hong Kong for the sun and surf book I'm working on. And, you'll never guess who's with us...yep, Sloan and Mark.

Holy crap, they're disgustingly cute together! I took a picture with my cell camera, check it out. Awwww... Now they look sweet and innocent napping together, but I have to let you in on the real deal, girlfriends.

Hanging out on this group for a while, I've heard some fantastically steamy stories, but you ladies are never going to believe what happened today. I'll let Sloan decide to share the deets if she wants, but I have to say, she's officially the queen of the Cougars and my personal hero.

Rachel: Oh, damn, that sounds cougarlicious. Give us a hint or two to hold us over! Did she complete the Challenge?

Lynn: Uh-huh. Big-time. I could tell by their goofy grins

this morning, but let's just say I might have even witnessed proof of it myself.

Darci: You tease! Are you four getting nasty together? You're both my heroes. Two hot hunks of Cougar bait at your beck and call, rawr!!!

Rachel: Bam chica wow wow. Go Sloan! Did you tell her about the other stuff, Lynn?

Lynn: Shhh, no. Not yet. Not like this.

Sloan: Looks like I picked a good time to dig out my laptop. What's going on here? Don't you ladies have your own Cougar bait to play with?

Darci: If it isn't our newest superstar member. Don't act all grumpy. We know you got banged until you were going off like a frog in a sock.

Sloan: Please tell me that's an Aussieism? Can someone translate?

Lynn snickered from across the aisle. She whispered, "It means something similar to going bananas. You know, as if a frog got stuck in a sock."

Sloan chuckled. "This has to be the best group of women in the world. Thank you for introducing me. I can't wait for the next Romanticon so we can hang out in person."

Sloan: Ah, Lynn explained, I got it now. Too funny. And, yep, that's pretty much how it was. God, he's amazing in bed and even better out of it. I can't wait to hang out at the beach this afternoon. I brought a ton of books.

Rachel: Have a great time, ladies. And, Lynn, you better fess up or we'll do it for you soon!

Lynn: You're right. It's the perfect opportunity. Let me do it my way, please. Oops, look at that. We're pulling into the station. Gotta go. Toodles!

Sloan glanced up when the train slowed. She shot Lynn a poignant look then snapped the lid of her computer closed.

"Uh-oh, what are you two up to?" Sebastian winced when Lynn cast him a beatific smile.

"Nothing. Why would you say that?"

"Because I know you, *mio amore*."

Lynn leaned over to kiss him until he forgot all about the calculating glint in his fiancé's eye.

Sloan couldn't be so easily distracted. What secret was the other woman keeping and how did it relate to her and Mark?

She swore she'd find out by the time they made it back to their apartments.

Chapter Seven

Sloan sighed as wind whipped her hair in front of her face. Mark stood behind her, his arms wrapped around her waist, keeping her steady as they flew over the waves in a huge, hydrofoil ferry.

The tourist transport vessel reminded her of her earlier study in contrasts. Garbage collectors lived in their work boats in Causeway Bay, which they'd departed from, surrounded by the high rise buildings in Hong Kong's financial district—some of the most amazing on Earth.

In the distance, she caught sight of a rich, green lump on the horizon. The blob quickly turned into a mixture of gray granite and lush vegetation swarmed by thousands of tiny fishing crafts, most barely bigger than a canoe. She swore she'd never seen so many boats in all her life. The bright, painted dinghies formed a mass tight enough to walk across, extending several hundred feet from the shore.

"The fishermen have all brought their early morning catches in for the dinner rush." Lynn spoke above the gusting air to fill her in.

"But it's not even lunchtime. Are there enough people living here to sustain all this?" She waved her hand toward the jumble.

"No. A bunch of the seafood will go back on this ferry to exclusive restaurants in Hong Kong for tonight's specials. Many of the people below deck are buyers. The ones who pay top dollar will score the cream of the crop. Though typically even the lower tiers are amazing here." Lynn licked her lips. "I'm looking forward to including a few dining recommendations in this section of the book. We might have to taste stuff from a handful of places."

"Now that's a sacrifice I'm willing to make," Sebastian remarked. He and Mark high-fived above the women's heads.

Before long, they disembarked into a port filled with more bicycles and insulated boxes. Merchants lined every inch of the boardwalk. They shouted about their amazing finds, bundled on the platform. The more elaborate set ups included aquariums stacked ten high to display their fish, still alive to guarantee freshness.

The vast array of creatures had Sloan questioning how anything could be left in the ocean if they repeated this ritual day after day. She fell behind as she examined the contents, picking out animals she'd only seen on National Geographic before. Cuttlefish, octopi, shellfish—they had them all.

Mark waited for her at the end of the walkway. He leaned one hip against a pylon with his arms crossed over his chest. God, he made her drool.

"You okay?" He cupped her face in one hand then kissed her.

"Mmm." She hugged him tight then took his hand in hers and started walking toward the shops where she spotted Lynn's bright sarong. "Yeah, hoping none of that goes to waste."

"I thought the same thing. Lynn told me they release the live fish that don't sell. But she might have said that to make me feel better." He shrugged. "She knows that kind of stuff bothers me."

Sloan beamed up at him. The more she learned about Mark, the more she felt she could be completely honest around him.

They wandered through the open air market, past the stalls of salted fish and souvenirs. Lynn darted into the spaces, returning with dozens of bags for Sebastian to carry, not that he seemed to mind. Nothing quite motivated Sloan to buy until they happened across a young woman. Quiet, she sat on a stool behind her wares, concentrating on her craft instead of shouting about bargains to anyone who wandered too close.

"See something you like?" Mark slowed to match her pace. They scanned the beautiful shell jewelry together.

When her gaze landed on a set of coordinating necklaces, one long and feminine, the other short and masculine, she didn't hesitate. "Excuse me?"

She hoped the woman would compensate for her ignorance. With the tourists flooding the island on a regular basis, she might know at least a little English.

When the girl looked up from her work, Sloan smiled.

"How much?" She raised the set in front of her then pointed to the calculator on the table beside a simple metal money box.

The jeweler looked between her and Mark then grinned. "Good for you."

Sloan and Mark turned to face each other, their gazes locked. Whether she was talking about the necklaces or their new relationship didn't matter.

The woman was right.

She punched a number in the four-operation calculator then spun it around. Three Hong Kong dollars.

Before Sloan could dig out her wallet, Mark beat her to it. He handed the woman a twenty then pointed to a pair of matching earrings and a bracelet. "Those too please."

When the merchant attempted to give him change, he refused.

"Thank you." He waved to the vendor before she could insist.

Beneath the spotty shade provided by a banyan tree, he gestured for Sloan to turn around. When she complied, he swept her hair from her neck then fastened the shell clasp. She spun in his arms, loving the appreciative flair in his eyes.

"Your turn." She stood on tip toes then reached up to secure the strand around his thick neck. What should have been simple knotted twine and strung shells looked gorgeous on him. Rugged, natural and unassuming.

"Perfect," they said at the same time.

"Jinx." He silenced her laugh with a scorching kiss.

Sloan couldn't say how long they indulged but it seemed like mere seconds before Sebastian's call cut through the haze of longing surrounding her. "There you two are. We've been searching up and down the market. Figures, you're more interested in making out than hunting trinkets."

"Sorry." Mark had to clear his throat a few times before he could say more. "What's next on the agenda?"

“I want to research the boatbuilding yard and the pirate’s cave but that probably means there’s no time for Pak Tai temple if we’re going to grab dinner on the beach before heading back.” Lynn scratched the attraction off her list.

“We could split up,” Mark suggested. “Not that I don’t want to hang out with you guys, but if it would help for the book, Sloan and I could check it out. You know, take some pictures and make notes for you to include.”

“You would do that?” Lynn clapped her hands but settled down after a moment. “You don’t have to. I know you don’t get too many breaks. If you want to hang out at the beach and relax that’s fine. I understand.”

“Really, I don’t mind if Mark doesn’t.” Sloan respected him for helping his friends. “I’d love to see a temple. What should we know about it?”

“Thank you, thank you, thank you. It’s the site of an annual bun festival that celebrates deities who protect the island’s inhabitants from the plague. In the early nineteenth century, locals believed the plagues were retribution for the evil deeds of the pirates who lived on the island. It’s supposed to be exquisite.”

“I think we can handle that.” Mark nodded.

“Well, there is the pesky part about it being inhabited by ghosts.”

“I don’t know, now I’m scared.” Sloan smiled. “I’ll assume they’re friendly ghosts.”

“If you see one, don’t wait to find out, okay?” Lynn laughed.

“I promise.” Mark crossed his heart.

“All right, kids, let’s get going. Meet at Tai Kwai Wan beach at, say, four o’clock?” Sebastian glanced at Lynn. “Is that long enough?”

“Depends on how many times they stop along the way to sneak a quickie.”

“Who cares about them?” Sebastian winked. “How many times are *we* going to stop for a quickie?”

“Ever done it in a pirate cave before, big guy?”

“Argggggh.” He lunged for Lynn.

She tossed a map to Mark then took off toward the boatbuilding yard. “See you guys later! Make sure you put sunscreen on any of your exposed parts!"

After consulting the chart, Mark led Sloan toward the peak of the island.

"Handy having a navigator along on vacation." She rested her head on his side, enjoying the weight of his arm around her waist as they strolled.

"Not something most people consider but thanks."

"I bet more women than you think have appreciated your skills." Sloan forced the truth between gritted teeth.

He didn't respond, content to enjoy the brilliant sun and their closeness. She didn't blame him. Hind-sighting wasn't high on her list of favorite activities either.

They stopped along the way to grab a plate of fantastic-looking shrimp and a couple bottles of local beer, which they inhaled under a striped umbrella as they watched a stream of people pass by. Even in a tourist village, many stared at her and Mark.

They stuck out like a sore thumb, especially with their blond hair. The attention unnerved her after a while and she got to her feet. "Ready to head to the temple?"

"Sure, let me grab another beer for the road. It's getting steamy out here. You want one?"

"Sure, thanks." Sloan smiled when he handed her a bottle. She used the condensation gathering on the cheap label to cool her neck.

Mark finished paying then turned back. He groaned when a droplet slid along her throat and leaned closer to lick the moisture from her skin. She shivered, her nipples hardening against his chest. He dropped a quick kiss on her lips then patted her ass. "We'd better move on before we get ourselves in trouble."

"Probably true." Still, she couldn't stop thinking about having him for dessert as they wound their way through the town.

They came to a crossroads in a residential neighborhood, turning toward the temple. A basketball court filled with kids adjoined the ancient monument. The juxtaposition struck a chord deep within her. How many children had grown up here, lived and died while the weathered fu dogs guarding the sacred space held eternal watch?

"Damn, that's something, isn't it?" Mark murmured below his breath but she caught it anyway.

"Spectacular." She entwined their fingers as they approached the building together. Magnificent enamel dragons perched on top of the red roof's peak. Inside, murals lined the walls and incense wafted on the breeze, perfuming the temple with its musk.

"You know..." Sloan immediately regretted breaking the silence.

"What?"

"Never mind."

"No. Tell me, Cougar. Please?"

"It's just that...well, I don't usually believe in things like ghosts." She winced, hoping he didn't think she'd gone nuts. "But, here, in this place, it's easy to imagine lost souls wandering these halls."

A bell tinkled in the distance, probably shifted by the breeze off the water.

"Sometimes I feel like a ghost."

His confession surprised the hell out of her.

Sloan stopped midstride, their linked arms forcing him to face her. "Why do you say that? Because of Sebastian?"

Mark nodded. "I'm a shitty friend, I know. But sometimes it's like I'm invisible."

"I see you."

"You're the first woman who's ever done that." Mark traced her eyebrow with one finger. "You make me feel special. I'm not the kind of guy who has to be the center of attention, you know? Most of the time I'm glad it's Sebastian in the limelight. I could never handle that circus day in, day out. But, for once—with you—it's nice to be the main event."

Sloan squeezed his hand, urging him to bend down so she could hold him. "You're the man I want, Marco. I haven't been this excited to spend time with someone...ever."

"Me either."

They smiled into each other's eyes before she broke the hushed intimacy.

"Have we seen enough for Lynn's notes?" She whispered in his ear, "I think it's time for one of those quickies."

"How about a longie instead?"

"Deal."

Hand in hand, they walked so fast they nearly jogged along the narrow streets toward the beach. Less popular than Tung Wan, which sat five hundred feet from the ferry pier and boasted the fabulous Warwick Hotel, Lynn had assured them Tai Kwai Wan held more natural beauty along with greater privacy, a combination Sloan appreciated.

As they rounded a bend in the road, the gorgeous landscape before Sloan stopped her in her tracks. The hill they stood on tumbled down to a wide, sandy beach. The greenery gave way to the sea on either side, as if the jungle hugged the ocean. In the distance, windsurfers darted beneath neon sails. Here and there, on the fringes of the beach, tiny bungalows on stilts dotted the coast.

Mark turned around to examine her, "Sorry, Cougar. It's getting hotter by the minute. I should have walked slower. Need a break?"

"No. I'm fine." She laughed. "I'm not *that* old."

He rolled his eyes.

"It's the view. I've never seen something this amazing."

He didn't look away from her. "I know what you mean."

"Stop that." She blushed.

"How do you feel about checking into one of those huts for the afternoon? You're going to burn to a crisp out in the sun all day." Mark ambled closer, trailing his fingertips across the tops of her breasts. "You're so…white."

"Thanks." Sloan burst out laughing. "I think. Though I'd kill for your Italian genes."

They headed for the giant, hand-painted sign with *Rental* scribbled in English below a string of Chinese characters. As they walked, they talked about their vastly different upbringings. She waited on the beach while he ran up to the stand.

Sloan could imagine Mark sailing along the Amalfi Coast, getting into trouble with Sebastian. They had a lifetime of experience as heartbreakers despite their youth. The unsettling flutter in her chest, which recurred each time she looked at him, made her afraid she would join the ranks of their casualties when the brilliant run she and Mark had going crashed and burned.

A worry for another day.

She couldn't help but reflect his grin as he neared her with a pile of towels and a bamboo bucket brimming with drinks.

"I scored the last one. Over there." He pointed to the most secluded bungalow. "Left a message for Sebastian and Lynn to join us when they arrive."

Though he couldn't have meant it the way it sounded, Sloan's imagination ran wild after the encounter on the train. When he caught the lascivious cast to her smile, he didn't freak out or make excuses for what he'd said.

Could he want to explore further?

Did she?

The thought had her desperate for something to cool her down. She kicked off her sandals, scooped them into her hand then sprinted for the shore, yelling over her shoulder, "Last one there has to be on the bottom."

The lack of a shark net at this beach made Sloan a little nervous, but she figured there were plenty of other tasty-looking people wading farther out than their bungalow. She splashed through the rising water until she was hip-deep. The crisp waves refreshed her, but they didn't do much to douse the flames building inside her.

By the time the ocean reached her waist, Mark overtook her. He managed to keep the towels dry and the pail out of the surf for the last twenty feet or so to their sanctuary. The straw structure had three walls. One covered the back, facing the beach, and each of the two sides. The front remained open, though sheers had been tied on either side for some privacy while maintaining the view from inside.

He lifted the supplies above his head, tucking them beneath the gauzy material, onto the floor of the bungalow, then returned to gloat.

Before he could start, she swung her arm and sent a curtain of water splashing in his direction. He shook the mist from his face, his hair swirling like a lush mane. She would have launched a second assault but he chose that moment to whip his shirt over his head and toss it into their hut, freezing her in place.

Her jaw hung open as she studied the flex of his contoured chest and shoulders, leaving her completely unprotected when he lunged for her, knocking them both beneath the waves.

Mark held her close as they tumbled through the jewel-blue water.

So strong, he propelled them upward still linked. Before they crested the surface, his mouth was on hers, kissing her, drowning her in pleasure.

Sloan gasped for air when his hand wandered from her back, over her ass then between her legs. His long fingers teased her pussy from behind, leaving her torn between rubbing against his palm or the hard shaft of his cock, which prodded her through his shorts.

"Don't make me wait, Marco," she moaned. "No more. Not after this morning and all afternoon. I can't take a minute more."

Chapter Eight

"Shit yes." He picked her up and threw her over his shoulder, causing a waterfall to pour over his body. His muscles glistened as he carried her to their hideout. He scaled the ladder, lashed to the stilts supporting the structure, with no difficulty then set her on the roughhewn floor, covered in reed mats.

His shorts disappeared in two seconds flat, leaving him proud and naked before her. She reached for his cock, but he deflected her hand, instead gripping the hem of her soaked tank and whipping it over her head.

He made quick work of undressing her, leaving only the necklace he'd bought her earlier. "Gorgeous."

"Not so bad yourself, lover boy."

"Now, about that loser-on-bottom thing…" He stalked closer. "I have to get inside you, Sloan."

"Yes." She spread her legs and played with her pussy. The pressure building wouldn't allow her to be patient.

"*Dio*, so sexy."

Mark crowded her until she took a step back and then another. Before she realized it, she tumbled toward the plush mattress lying on the floor. Her lover caught her, slowing her descent but following her down, covering her with his powerful form.

His bare skin glided across hers, stroking her diamond-hard nipples and caressing her belly with his firm abdomen.

"Yes, yes, yes." She couldn't say more but she clawed at his shoulders, encouraging him to sink deeper into her welcoming hold.

His lips flew across her mouth, her neck and her chest, licking, sucking and kissing anywhere he could reach. He plumped the heavy weight of her breasts in his large hands. "Your tits are perfect."

"Fuck them."

Mark didn't balk. He knelt on either side of her torso then placed the dripping head of his cock in her cleavage. Sloan gathered her breasts in her hands then squished them together, enfolding him in their soft warmth. He shuddered above her then began to thrust until the thick head poked from between the mounds of flesh.

Sloan tilted her head to suck the tip each time it appeared, easing his way and lubricating his shaft. The weight of his balls dragging across her torso turned her on. When he noticed her squirming beneath him, desperate, he pulled out then flipped her around.

His strangled groan served as a testament to the effort it took him to pause.

She opened her mouth to ask why he'd stopped. He took it as a cue and plunged his cock inside the moist orifice. Instinct had her swallowing around his length—salty and hard. She sucked him deep until he buried his face between her thighs and returned the favor, lapping her from clit to ass.

"Mmmph." The mass of his cock muffled her shout.

Mark rolled to his back, propping her on her hands and knees, giving her free rein to fuck his face with her pussy. She took advantage of the opportunity, squirming in his hold until his mouth landed in the perfect position. One of his hands migrated from palming her ass to snake around her waist. His arm locked there, pinning her in place, ensuring he could reach the syrup dripping from her.

Each time he hit a particularly sensitive spot with his tongue, she sucked him harder, teaching him with her feedback. Soon, she realized the error of her ways. She couldn't stop the tsunami of sensation barreling down on her no matter how badly she wanted to wait and come with her student inside her.

He moaned encouragement, vibrating her clit. The stimulation shattered her restraint. Her body tensed then flailed, thrusting in shallow arcs as he chased her with his tongue, ensuring the full extent of her pleasure.

The initial euphoria faded, leaving her limp in his supportive grasp. She realized she still sucked on his cock with gentle pulls that echoed the pulsing of her pussy.

Her young lover shifted her off him, withdrawing from her mouth.

"Thank you, Marco," she whispered, unable to catch her breath.

"Roll on your side, Cougar. I want you to share this view with me." He growled the command. When she took longer than he preferred, he collared her waist with his hands and adjusted her until her ass snugged to his crotch and they both faced the idyllic scenery. He aligned his hips behind her, fitting the blunt tip of his massive hard-on to her opening.

He pillowed her head on his biceps, his other hand stroking her ribs, her breasts, her tummy and her ass. Everywhere she wished he would pay attention to, he did, as though he could read her mind. She rotated her head toward him and he captured her parted lips.

His endless caresses rekindled her lust.

Mark explored the inner reaches of her mouth, licking her gums, her tongue and her palate. She gasped against his lips when he flexed his pelvis, feeding her his cock inch by inch from behind. Still, he never stopped kissing her, nipping the corner of her mouth, cupping her cheek.

His balls tapped against her when he bottomed out in her pussy.

"Sloan!" He panted against her cheek. "I have to fuck."

"Yes, Marco." She braced herself on the mattress with one arm then lifted her top leg. He caught it behind the knee, spreading her farther. His cock sank in a bit deeper, making them both cry out.

Sloan allowed herself to be carried away. She lost track of where the motion they generated merged with the ebb and flow of the ocean, which stretched out before them on the other side of the gauzy curtain.

The length of Mark's shaft delved to the root with every tender, slow thrust before he withdrew it completely. The instant it penetrated the tight ring of muscle at her entrance once more she saw fireworks on the horizon. Sparks shot along her spine, straight to her clit.

A little more and she would come apart. Her entire body strained in his hold, arching to maximize the impact of his veiny shaft on her sensitized channel, fusing them together. When she shifted her hand, he released her leg then covered her fingers with his on her clit. He studied the motion she used on herself for the span of several heartbeats before taking over on his own.

Sloan held her leg high so he could work her both from the rear and in front, trapping her in a vise of bliss. Rapture fizzled along her nerve endings. But his ragged cries, as he chanted her name, alerted her to his impending orgasm, instigating her climax.

The first wash of his hot come on her swollen tissue amplified her initial contractions until she screamed her relief. He locked her in his arms as he filled her to overflowing with the semen he released in burst after burst. His cock still jerked inside her when he lowered his mouth to her neck and nipped her beside his necklace in a show of possession so primal her pussy hugged him tight again.

And again.

And again.

* * * * *

A few hours later—hours filled with lounging, laughter and more loving—some very obvious splashing and thunderous discussion alerted them to Lynn and Sebastian's approach long before their friends reached their paradise hideaway.

"Thanks for the heads-up but we're decent in here," Mark shouted, his voice rich with laughter.

"You know, I don't object to indecency." Sebastian boosted his fiancé into the open-fronted bungalow with one arm then handed her a picnic basket and a cheap cooler. "I just want to make sure we're invited, not crashing the party."

"You're always welcome, *amico*." Mark smiled at Sebastian

and Lynn, who glanced toward Sloan.

She nodded as well. "I'm glad to see you escaped the pirates."

"No thanks to this saucy wench." Sebastian slapped Lynn on the ass as she bent over to unpack the amazing dinner they'd brought.

World-class food served on banana leaves, eaten cross-legged on a mattress in a straw hut, in the company of great friends—Sloan couldn't believe her good fortune.

After a delicious meal and bunches of stories about their day apart, they packed all the garbage in a plastic bag.

"Could you hand me a drink?" Sloan asked Sebastian, who sprawled closest to the supplies.

"I think we're all out, babe. Sorry, I should have grabbed more. I didn't realize how dehydrated we'd gotten today. Make one last beer run with me, Mark?" Sebastian put the lid on the cooler then tucked it under his arm.

"Sure." Mark winked at her. "We worked up quite a sweat before. Don't want my Cougar to run out of steam."

He kissed her on the cheek before taking off at a run, launching himself—still shirtless—into the sea.

The guys cannonballed off the platform into the water, wrestling each other while they whooped and hollered like a pair of kids, making their way toward the restaurant on the shore.

When Sloan quit shaking her head, she turned to Lynn. "Thanks for dinner. You didn't have to buy. Hell, inviting me on this trip was more than I could have hoped for. Today has been wonderful."

"My pleasure, it's the least I could do after your help in researching the temple. Not to mention the show you two put on for us this morning."

"I'm glad it didn't freak you out." Sloan turned to face Lynn head-on. "I've never done anything like that before."

"Look, Sloan, I realize things have moved at the speed of light since you and I ran into each other at the stadium the other day, but none of us will judge you. Hell, I fucked Sebastian less than two hours after meeting him. Not too much longer after that I was sandwiched between him and Mark." Lynn clapped her hand over her mouth. "Oh my God. What am I saying? I didn't think. Shit. Are you okay with that?"

"Um, yeah. It's fine. Except, I'm super jealous." Sloan raised one eyebrow. "Mark mentioned the incident on the phone the other night. I hope you don't mind him sharing. I told him the idea of two guys screwing around was a big fantasy of mine and he said he'd experimented with you two. He couldn't believe how much it turned him on when you asked him to play with Sebastian's ass."

Sloan's face flamed but she found she couldn't lie. Didn't want to. The possibility of realizing her wicked lusts subdued the last hint of shyness she possessed.

"I trust you, Sloan. So I'll tell you a little secret. On the blog earlier, the girls were referring to it anyway. They'll spill tonight if I chicken out." Lynn grinned. "Ever since that night on the plane, Sebastian has been curious. We've fooled around with…toys."

It made Sloan more comfortable to see Lynn off balance, exactly like she felt.

"Are you saying—" She held her breath, afraid to do anything to keep her new friend from continuing her revelation.

"Yes. We've been working our way up. It started with Mark. What, six…eight…months ago now? After that, I noticed Sebastian got off faster when I fingered his ass while I went down on him." The other woman scooted closer and lowered her voice to a whisper though no one could possibly hear. "One day, when I had him tied up and blindfolded, I used my smallest vibrator on him as I sucked his cock. He went berserk. After that, he ordered a set of butt plugs from a shop on the internet. He enjoys wearing one when we screw around."

"Jesus, that's hot."

"I know. And it gets better." Lynn took a deep breath then confessed, "Last month, he gave me a strap-on for my birthday."

"He did not!"

"He did." She beamed. "He *loves* it when I fuck him."

"Wow." Sloan's eyes widened. She didn't know if she could imagine doing that to Mark, but then again, she'd never dreamed of giving a man a blowjob while on a train either.

"I mean, it's not like we do it all the time, and I think Bastian would be fine with messing around with me every once in a while, but both of us have wondered what it would be like to have another threesome. Maybe a foursome? To go all the way this time." Lynn paused before continuing. "The only man Sebastian trusts enough to consider is Mark."

A cascade of moisture flooded Sloan's pussy.

"Do you think he'd be into it?" Lynn chewed her lower lip. "Would you? I don't want to mess up what you two have going. I know it's new, fresh, and I would hate myself if we interfered—"

"Stop." Sloan leaned closer to hug the other woman. "I'm flattered you asked my opinion in the first place. You know Marco so much better than I do. You're freaking yourself out over nothing. Your…proposition…sounds like one of the sexiest things I could imagine. And for the record, I think Mark would be extremely interested."

Lynn flopped onto her back on the mattress. "Oh thank God."

Sloan joined the woman. The promise of something so decadent and forbidden left her weak and boneless. "You know, I probably shouldn't say anything, but—"

"After all I shared, don't you dare hold back."

"Fair enough." Sloan laughed then sighed. "I've been aware of Mark for a long time, but it's been only a couple days since I really started to get to know him. So take this with a grain of salt."

"Time doesn't matter." Lynn shook her head as a soft smile crossed her face. "Bastian's mom told me that when I first started dating him, and she was right. When you meet your mate, you know them. Right away. I don't want to curse you two, but I can't mistake how you and Mark are together. It's a perfect partnership. If you have a gut instinct about him, go with it. It's probably right."

Sloan nodded. "Mark feels inferior to Sebastian. Like a second-class citizen in their friendship."

"What!" The other woman bolted upright. "How can that be? We love him. Bastian is closer to him than a brother. There's no way we would ever disrespect him like that."

"Shush, I don't think it has anything to do with you two. It's more that Sebastian captures all the glory in the league." Sloan shrugged. "I think years of playing second fiddle have started to make him doubt his worth. It would mean a lot to him if Sebastian shared himself. You know, let Mark drive for once."

"He's been hurting yet he hasn't said anything." Lynn bit her lip and Sloan caught the sheen of tears in the other woman's eyes. "He never would have either. Damn him and his noble streak. We would have made things right. Did you know Sebastian is the only driver in the league who splits his winnings evenly with his navigator?"

"I didn't, but that's very generous."

"In the months I've known Bastian, he's woken up in a sweaty mess about half a dozen times in the middle of the night. He has a recurring nightmare about crashing. So do I, but this is different. He's terrified that he'll do something while driving, cause an accident." Lynn's eyes shone with the fear all race wives endured. "He doesn't care about himself. He obsesses about injuring Mark, or worse. I think he'd love to let go of the burden of control for a night or two every once in a while. It weighs heavy on him."

"Damn, they're so close and still so secretive. I'm glad we talked." Sloan covered Lynn's shaking hand. "And that you invited me to be a part of all this."

"Mark chose you. Smartest thing he's done. I've been around him every day for months but I didn't notice what you did in an instant. You get him. You're looking straight into his heart and you like what you see."

"*Like* might be an understatement."

"I hope so." Lynn hugged her. "For both your sakes."

"I think we can make this work for everyone."

"I do too, Sloan." After a minute or two of reflective silence, Lynn laughed.

Sloan raised an eyebrow in her direction.

"The Cougar Challenge ladies are going to be *so* jealous."

"Damn straight. Go us!"

"Rawr!"

Chapter Nine

During the taxi ride from the ferry back to the train station in Hong Kong, Sloan's cell phone started buzzing, flashing and ringing like mad. It could only mean one thing.

"Shit, someone stirred up a hornet's nest." She dug in her purse until she snagged the offensive device, aligning her mind to business and away from her holiday.

"You need to get here. Now." Her assistant sounded frazzled, an uncommon occurrence.

"On my way, how bad is it?"

"Really bad."

"Shit. Hold things together until I get in. About two hours."

"Will do. But it's not the usual—"

Crap, her cell must have been searching for a signal the entire time they were on Cheung Chau. She'd drained the battery. It died before she'd finished receiving her assistant's message.

"Damn it!"

"An emergency?" Mark took her hand in his. "If one of the guys did something stupid, I'm going to kick his ass. I was looking forward to spending a quiet night in with you."

Lynn exchanged a meaningful look with her.

"Same here." Sloan grimaced. "Probably not going to happen now. Sorry."

"It's not your fault, Cougar." He patted her hand. "I'll be waiting whenever you're ready."

Closer to three hours later, because of the unflagging traffic in the city—she'd never figure out how they managed to jam five cars wide in two lanes—they jogged into the international housing complex.

Mark and Sebastian strode side by side, each with their woman on their arm. Sloan expected them to part ways and head upstairs, but her friends stayed close on her heels when she angled toward the office space she'd been using for official business.

Their support touched her.

But it made it that much worse when she opened the glass door and recognized the irate man shouting at her poor assistant.

She tripped, landing in Mark's secure embrace. The room spun as several things happened at once. Lynn and Mark kept asking if she was okay as Sebastian stepped in front of her, blocking the advance of the man who'd waited on her to return.

"Where the hell have you been?" Larry didn't seem to notice the illness swamping her gut. No surprise there, it'd always been all about him. "I flew halfway around the fucking world to see you and you couldn't show up any quicker?"

Why now? After all this time, her bastard ex-husband had to choose this day—the best day of her life—to ruin.

"Wh-what do you want?" She peeked around Mark and Sebastian's intimidating forms.

"Give me another chance…*sweetie*." The red splotches on his cheeks made it hard to take him serious.

"Hang on. Is this tool your ex?" Mark transformed in an instant. His chest puffed up and his shoulders dropped back. He cracked his knuckles. From affable and gentle to protector in half a second. God, that made her moist.

"Yeah." Larry confirmed his suspicions. "I mean, I'm her husband. Not a tool."

"*Ex*-husband," she whispered.

"Do you want to talk to this asshole?" Sebastian looked to Sloan for confirmation.

She hesitated as she recalled all the sleepless nights she'd spent vacillating between outrage and regret. She'd sworn, if she had a chance to do things differently, she would have made sure her husband had what he needed, that he hadn't had to turn to the comfort of others.

But that was before she'd accepted the truth.

No matter what she did or did not do, she couldn't control Larry's behavior. If he had loved her, he would have worked things out instead of lying and cheating. An honorable man would have broken things off, if it came to that, before screwing around.

Mark had shown her what a caring lover should look like.

Larry could never match up.

If she scoured her soul, she knew she'd find she never truly loved him. Her heart had never ached after two seconds apart from him as it did for Mark. She never remembered losing herself to pleasure and drifting in the shelter of his arms as she had with Mark.

Mark was the man she needed to talk to.

"No." She turned away. "There's nothing left to say."

"Wait! Sloan, please." A fat tear dropped from Larry's bloodshot eyes. Had he been drinking again? Unfortunately for him, the sight inspired no sympathy in her. "I fucked up. I know it now. I didn't appreciate you. I…I miss you."

His pathetic attempt to lure her had zero effect.

"I'm sorry. I can't do this." Sloan brushed past everyone, crashing into the door hard enough it smacked against the wall outside then bounced back, the handle banging into her hip. It would leave a bruise but she hardly noticed, her entire body numb.

At the end of the hallway, someone exited the elevator. She dashed for the closing doors, waving her hand to keep them from shutting as she slipped inside. Her eyes widened when she saw Mark less than two steps behind her in the mirrored wall of the car.

He tapped the up arrow and had the doors opening once more.

"Damn, you're quick when you're upset." He reached for her. Slow, steady, he gave her a chance to evade his touch.

Nothing could have been further from her mind. She launched herself into his spread arms, soaking in the comfort of his embrace. Larry's sudden appearance had shocked her, leaving her no time to think or respond to his ridiculous plea with the snappy comebacks she'd crafted for months while she nursed her wounded pride.

None of that mattered now.

Sloan prayed for the doors to shut so she could be alone with Mark—attempt to explain the jumble of emotions overwhelming her—but someone slapped the button again, preventing their assent.

"Sloan? What the hell is this?" Larry glared in their direction. "I thought I was the moron, fucking around with women half my age. What are you thinking? You know what, it doesn't matter. You've had your fun. Now come home with me."

"My home is here." She squeezed Mark's supportive hand.

"With this kid? Grow up, Sloan. You'll come back to your senses, like I did. I can't guarantee I'll be waiting when you decide you want a man."

"Mark's more of a man than you'll ever be, jackass."

"And I'd never be foolish enough to let my Cougar go." Mark tucked her against his chest then stared at Larry's finger, which continued to depress the elevator button. "I suggest you take your hand off that if you'd like to keep it in one piece, gramps."

When Larry would have argued, Sebastian stepped in, shielding them from his sight. Several other crew members spotted the commotion and joined the driver to create a damn effective wall. They crowded Larry until he relented, abandoning the controls.

Sloan chuckled as the narrowing gap between the closing elevator doors obscured Larry's sputtering face. She tossed him a finger wave before turning to Mark, her smile dimming as she considered his declaration. "Did you mean that?"

"Yeah." He stepped closer then picked her up as though he needed to hold her as much as she craved the comfort of his embrace.

She wrapped her legs around his waist and her arms around his shoulders so they could see each other eye to eye.

"I've always had a thing for you, Sloan. Some part of me recognized you were meant to be mine even when I didn't think I had a chance at claiming you. But...are you sure? I'm betting you spent a lot of time wishing your husband would grovel like this—that you would make him suffer but ultimately forgive him."

"How do you know?"

"Because my heart understands you. You wouldn't read all those romance novels if you didn't hope for a happily ever after of your own." He shifted his grip to cradle her while staring deep into her eyes. "Be sure, Sloan. If you still have feelings for him—"

"I don't."

"Then how did he impact you so strongly down there?" Mark frowned, the expression so atypical for him, his mouth couldn't quite pull it off. "It killed me to see you run like that—"

"He didn't." She silenced his objections with a soft kiss. "He startled me. Worse, I frightened and disgusted myself. How could I have given so much of my life to a man I don't love? Never did. The waste of time is horrifying. I feel *nothing* for him."

"And for me?" Mark did a good job of masking his hope. His fear. But she saw right through the brave façade.

Could she take the risk? Change her life? Shift gears?

Sloan rubbed their noses together then whispered, "Everything for you."

"Yes, *Dio*." He swallowed so hard she heard it. "It's the same for me, Cougar."

She wrapped her arms around his neck and kissed him until stars danced in her vision.

"I…" Sloan stalled. What could she say? She wished she could assure him this time it was the real thing but the promise stuck in her throat. She'd made the mistake of jumping into a relationship once before. Repeating history would destroy her, no matter how tempting her young stud made it.

"Shh. I don't expect any vows, not after a few days of fooling around. I don't need them because I know. For the first time in my life, I'm certain I've found what I need. In myself. In you."

"I want to believe it too." She kissed him. Gentle. Tender. When they arrived on their floor, he walked them to his room without putting her down. "I feel more for you than I have words for. But I need time, Mark. To be sure—"

"As long as it takes, Sloan." He smiled as he nuzzled the hair at her temple. "I'm not going anywhere. And neither are you,

Cougar."

"Not even inside? There's a nice big bed in there. A tub full of jets too." She peeked over his shoulder as she rubbed her pussy across the bulge in his pants. "I need a place to hide from my psycho ex-husband for several hours, until he gives up and slinks away. Why don't you try to convince me some more?"

"I like the sound of that. But it won't be very hard." Mark's newfound confidence fired her blood. Then left her speechless when he dropped the bomb. "You're going to love me. As much as I love you."

When she would have sputtered some meaningless, reflexive objection, Mark hijacked her mouth and swallowed her fear. In the heat of his all-consuming passion, she melted and let him have his way.

Defeat had never tasted so good.

* * * * *

A knock at the connecting door to Sebastian and Lynn's room drew Mark and Sloan from the action movie they watched late on Sunday evening.

"Come in, it's open," Mark shouted from the bed, too relaxed to move.

"Hey, we heard Larry was escorted to the airport. The crew confirmed he's off the continent. Left on the nine o'clock flight." Lynn and Sebastian walked, hand in hand, to perch on the edge of the mattress. "We came to see if you're all right."

"Relieved." Sloan held out her arms and the pair closed the gap. "Thank you for letting me know."

The group exchanged hugs all around. Knowing his friends would protect Sloan filled Mark with gratitude.

"Everything's good." Sloan nodded toward the couple who gauged the atmosphere.

Something was…off.

Sebastian and Lynn hovered as though they expected Sloan to make a move or something. Instead she said, "But I didn't approach Mark about…what we discussed. I didn't have time or the energy to handle it alone. Sorry."

Uh-oh, he didn't know if he liked the sound of that.

"Don't apologize, babe." Sebastian stroked Sloan's hair then dropped a quick peck on her cheek. "I should have done it myself anyway."

The sight of Sebastian's tan skin against Sloan's pale delicacy made Mark long for the days when he'd shared women with Bastian. He would have enjoyed gifting her with the pleasure two men could impel. Before his imagination could run with the thought, his best friend shocked the hell out of him.

"But, in that case, I need to talk to you about something, *amico*." Sebastian didn't tip-toe around. He snatched the remote, clicked off the movie then met Mark's stare directly.

Mark *definitely* didn't like that.

Sloan took one of his hands in hers and Lynn grabbed the other.

"Holy shit, who died?" Panic threatened to overrule his calm.

"Nothing like that." Sebastian's strangled laugh confused him further.

"Then spit it out already." Mark would have tugged on his hair if he'd had his hands free.

"Fuck." Bastian looked to the women for encouragement then paced away and back. "This is harder than I thought."

Mark growled a warning.

"Okay. Son of a bitch. Here it is." Sebastian inhaled so deep his breath might have expanded his toes. "Remember when I first met Lynn and the three of us got together on the jet?"

Mark's cock rose to instant attention. Would Sloan freak if she noticed?

He stared at a spot on the wall across the room from him and tried to will the arousal inspired by the memory to fade, but his stubborn hard-on firmed further.

Sloan giggled from his side then cupped his cheek in her palm. She angled his face toward her then kissed him with a brush of her lips, lighter than a butterfly. "Don't start pretending now, Marco. You told me how horny it made you to touch them both."

Holy shit, he'd never spoke of the incident with Sebastian and Lynn. Not since that night. Admitting his extra-dirty streak freaked him out. He ended up one-down from Sebastian enough. He didn't need to add this to the pile.

"So you guys are trying to ambush me?" He leapt from the bed, putting his back to the wall.

"No, *amico.* That's not it at all." Sebastian held his hands out and inched toward Mark. The navigator took baby steps backward until his shoulders hit the solid surface behind him. "It's… I wondered if you were interested in experimenting a little more. Our Cougars are hot to watch us. Together. They promise they'll make it worth our while. Imagine. A foursome, Marco. With the women we love. And each other."

"You thought that if you all ganged up on me, I'd bend over for Bastian?" He accepted the panic and rage overtaking him as though he were a bull facing down a matador but he couldn't contain it a moment longer. Not after all this time. He swept the glasses and ice bucket from the table by his side. "Like always!"

"They were right." Sebastian halted the cycle of anger, betrayal and humiliation spiraling out of control when he staggered as through sucker-punched, one hand clutching his chest. Lynn rushed to Bastian's side, shooting Mark a look that flipped between regret and anger for hurting her mate. "How did I miss it? I had *no idea* you felt like that."

"Fuck." Mark spun, slapping his palms on the wall then attempting to regain mastery of his bellowing breath. The comfort of Sloan's delicate grasp encircled his waist. She rested her check on his spine. Having her near leached his anger, replacing it with shame. "I'm sorry, Bastian."

He looked over his shoulder at the man smothering his fiancé in a desperate embrace. Despite everything bubbling to the surface, Mark still cared. He hadn't intended to hurt the other man. Sebastian wasn't to blame for Mark's moronic insecurities. He crossed to his friend then knocked him on the shoulder.

"It's not you. You've never treated me as anything but a brother, more than. It's the rest of the world that's the problem." He glanced up at the two women in the room. Big mistake. Both had giant diamond tears sparkling on their pretty cheeks.

Sebastian released Lynn then clapped Mark on the back in a double-armed clinch; he chose not to think of it as a hug. "I should have seen how it ate at you. I should have stopped it. Let me make it up to you."

"That's not necessary." *And impossible.* Mark shook his head but Sebastian kept talking.

"I haven't been able to scrub that night on the jet out of my mind. When you touched me." Sebastian shuddered. "It drove me insane. Lynn and I have been…fooling around…but it's not the same. I'm curious."

Mark hated to disappoint the other man but, no matter how skilled Sebastian might be in bed, he wasn't going to fix this with a couple of stellar orgasms at the price of Mark's last shred of dignity.

No way.

"I can't do that with you." Mark feared losing his best friend when he saw the disappointment crushing Sebastian. "The thought of being fucked in the ass doesn't do it for me. I'm so sorry. If I would let anyone, I'd let you. I just…can't."

"You still don't understand." Sebastian tilted his head then spelled it out. "I'm asking *you* to fuck *me*. Please, *amico*."

Chapter Ten

"You want *me* to fuck *you*?" Mark couldn't believe his ears.

He looked to Sloan then Lynn to see if anyone else had heard the insanity Bastian spouted, but both women seemed eager for his response. Hopeful and excited.

What the hell? Sure, he'd thought about it a million times since the night six months ago when he'd lost it all over Bastian's shin, but he'd tried to put it out of his mind, convince himself the thrill stemmed from something novel. Something freaky they'd never tried.

God knew, there weren't a lot of things left in that category.

But now they both stood face-to-face, giant wood straining the front of their sweats.

"Yeah." Bastian couldn't seem to say more than that. Mark couldn't blame the man. All the extra blood in the driver's body must have rushed between his legs to produce the mammoth erection tenting the front of his pants.

Holy shit, Bastian wasn't joking—wasn't offering simply to make up for some imagined slight. He really wanted to try this.

"Whoa." Mark plopped onto the bed. Bad idea since it put him at eye level with Sebastian's full cock. "And you two are okay with it?"

He spun to face Sloan, noting the spots of heat on her cheeks. Her nipples formed visible bumps beneath her nightgown.

Lynn broke the silence. "Sloan and I think it's one of the

most provocative ideas we could dream up."

"We read about stuff like this but never imagined we'd be…"

"So lucky."

Now they finished each other's sentences? Oh fuck, he and Bastian were in deep shit.

"Mmm." He recognized the aroused moan from Sloan.

The attraction radiating from the three people he cared about most started to affect him. His heart raced, pumping blood to inflate his half-hard cock at record speed. "Tonight?"

"Right now," Sebastian insisted. "I can't stand the wait. I've been avoiding asking for months. Don't make me wonder. Yes or no, Mark?"

"Yes." The word flew from his lips without thought.

Before he could retract it, Sebastian released a stream of curses interspersed with prayer in rapid-fire Italian then whipped his jogging pants to his ankles. He stepped out of the slippery fabric, leaving himself exposed. Not the first time Mark had seen all of his friend, but the only time he'd imagined touching him with intent instead of the contact that occurred due to the proximity of their bodies during a threesome.

Not that those accidental caresses had disgusted him. Far from it.

Sebastian rummaged through the pockets of the garment, tossed a tube of lube on the bed then dropped the pants to the floor along with his shirt and socks, immediately forgotten.

"Come up here, Bastian." Lynn encouraged her fiancé to climb onto the bed beside her. The sight of their fierce kiss aroused Mark further. He noticed Sloan looking on, fascinated. Her fingers had latched on to her distended nipple.

Oh holy mother of all wicked dreams, this had the potential to be the best night of his life. Still, he refused to jeopardize his budding relationship. "Will this change how you feel about me, Sloan? Us?"

"Only to make me want you more." She licked her finger then swirled it around the satin-covered point until the fabric grew damp and translucent. "I'm so wet right now I think I need a towel."

"No." The objection came from Lynn, startling them all. "I have a better idea."

She lay on her back on the bed, her feet hanging off the end, her knees bent at the edge of the mattress. "I'm going to suck Bastian while Mark prepares him."

Mark couldn't say who groaned loudest.

"Let Bastian take care of Sloan." Lynn winked at her. "He has a very skilled mouth."

"Are you okay with that?" Sloan checked in with Mark.

"*Dio*, yes." The possibility had him hard as a rock. "Find pleasure however you can. It's always thrilled me to watch him satisfy our women. I didn't think I'd be able to share that with you."

He looked to Lynn, who smiled up at them. "Thank you."

"No, thank you." She licked her lips. "You have no idea how bad I want to watch you fuck Bastian. I could come from thinking about it. Hell, I *have* come while imagining it."

She slithered free of her dress while they observed then trailed her fingers along the center of her body until her fingers buried in her pussy.

Mark shot a glance at Sloan, impressed to see her taking it all in, not averting her gaze from Lynn. A true connoisseur of all things pleasurable, Sloan seemed to appreciate Lynn's sensuality.

"You're lucky, Bastian." Sloan smiled at his best friend. "Lynn's one smoking Cougar."

Sebastian couldn't answer when his woman crooked her finger. Instead, he jumped to obey her command. He knelt with one leg on either side of her shoulders then fed his fiancé his cock.

Sloan and Mark both stared at the licentious display. When Bastian dipped his torso, reaching behind him to spread his ass, his shoulders hit the bed and he turned his face to rest on the duvet.

"Wow."

He couldn't have said it better than Sloan. Nestled in the pucker of Bastian's ass, an anal plug stretched his friend's hot hole.

Sloan leaned in for a better view, petting Bastian's flank as Mark approached the end of the bed. Sebastian moaned when she trailed a finger around the base of the object. Mark wondered what it felt like, so he mimicked her exploration.

Bastian glided his cock between his fiancé's lips, rocking into Mark and Sloan's questing fingers on each back stroke. With his free hand, Mark grabbed his cock through his clothes, priming it. The tingle in his balls proclaimed it a bad idea if he wanted to last long enough to push inside his friend's virgin ass.

"I don't think I can take this slow, Bastian."

Mark panted as he tugged on the base of the embedded device. It resisted exiting Sebastian's clenched ring of muscle until he increased the pressure. Then it slipped free, revealing a spread orifice that tempted him to surround his cock in its heat.

All the while, Sloan riled both him and Bastian with a series of caresses that drove him nuts. When she reached over to pinch Mark's nipple through his shirt, his entire body sang. She peeked up at him.

"What do you want, Sloan?"

"Can I put you inside him?" She ratcheted his arousal higher with her request.

Lynn moaned, inspiring a curse from Sebastian at the vibration. The tips of the other woman's fingers came into view as she fondled her lover's balls.

"Yes, yes." Excitement overwhelmed Mark, damning him to immobility.

"Then you better get naked. Quick." Sloan snapped him out of it.

Mark ripped off his pants as he peeled his shirt away. By the time the cotton hit the carpet, Sloan had wrapped her dainty fist around his shaft and aimed the head of his erection at Bastian's ass.

He could thrust inside in a nanosecond. The forbidden channel beckoned him, the opening contracting as Sebastian jabbed his cock into Lynn's mouth with tiny strokes.

"Are you ready?" Sloan took over, pacing the encounter when Mark could not. She painted Bastian's entrance with the fluid dripping from the head of Mark's cock then added a generous drizzle of lubrication.

Both men shuddered at the cool gel moisturizing their skin.

"Yes." Bastian huffed then got bossy, a hint of the man they knew and loved seeping through his submissive offering. "Feed me his cock then put your soaked pussy under my mouth before I explode. It's not going to be a marathon affair. Not this time."

"I don't think you're the only one about to blow." All four of them struggled to control their breathing.

When they chatted too long, Lynn reached around and smacked Bastian's ass. Hard.

"Not helping," he growled.

"Hurry." Mark and Sebastian said in unison.

Sloan wrapped her fingers tighter around Mark's erection then guided him toward his target. He sank the barest amount inside Bastian's tight, scalding passage and feared he'd shoot right then and there. His head tipped backward and the tendons in his neck tensed until they raised prominently.

When he lodged in the constricting muscle, Sloan encouraged him to reverse his motion then plunge forward again as she glazed him with more lube. The strength of Bastian's initial resistance surprised Mark. How tight had his friend been before the toy?

The thought made his muscles twitch, ramming him through the final barrier. He sank halfway into Bastian's ass. Sebastian grunted below him and Sloan whispered soothing praise as she stroked his back, his shoulders, his neck.

Mark infiltrated bit by bit until his abdomen rested on Sebastian's flank. He couldn't believe the sight before him—Bastian writhing as he accepted Mark's entire shaft, surrendering to his wishes. Loving his supplication and begging for more with twitches of his ass. Rampant lust assaulted Mark, driving him crazy with ecstasy. But the fantasy wasn't complete.

"Sloan, move up there. Let Bastian service you." Mark fucked Bastian with one long, hard lunge when his Cougar spread her legs on either side of the man's head.

"Eat her, *amico*." Mark fucked steady and strong now, relishing the moans, curses and entreaties that fell from his friends' lips. "Do a good job and I'll fill you with my come."

Sebastian didn't wait to hear more. He gripped Sloan's upper thighs and dragged her into position. His lips latched around her clit and he sucked. His throat worked as he flicked his tongue over the pretty pink lips and sipped the honey from her drenched folds.

Without additional direction, he buried two fingers in Sloan's pussy. Each reintroduction of Mark's cock into the man's virgin ass spurred Sebastian to pay it forward to Sloan, driving his hand into her saturated pussy.

"Bastian, you feel so fucking good. So hot. Tight. Rough. Solid. Different." Mark felt Lynn's thighs tense at his description. He assumed she played with herself as she sucked Sebastian, his friend…his lover.

Mark decided to torture the woman. Next time he'd ensure she had a ringside seat for the show. "Can't believe we never did this before. I could fuck you all day long. Do you like it when I ram deep?"

He demonstrated with a couple fierce poundings of his hips, secure in his faith of Bastian's durability.

Sebastian grunted then devoured Sloan's pussy, communicating in a primal language they all understood.

"Good. I like banging you hard. You can take it, right, *amico?*"

The entire bed shook when Lynn climaxed beneath them without warning. She writhed between his legs, inspiring Mark to move faster—vigorous and demanding.

"Shit yes!" Sebastian lifted his head for two seconds. "Use teeth, Lynn. Come with my cock in your mouth."

Lynn continued to orgasm with round after round of cries and moans. Mark kept fucking, building his pace, his intensity. He wrapped his hands around Sebastian's waist. So much firmer, wider, than Sloan's.

Mark didn't have to hold anything in reserve. Instead, he shuttled inside the smooth tissue, trying to ignore the sweat rolling down his nape with the effort of suppressing his orgasm.

"Oh yeah," Mark shouted when Bastian's ass gripped him tighter. "You're about to shoot, aren't you?"

He picked up the pace, forging double time into the forbidden territory. The ridge surrounding his cock head snagged on the contracting ring of muscle at Sebastian's entrance. Over and over.

"Ye—" Sebastian didn't make it further than that before his entire body halted and he roared into Sloan's drenched core. He poured his semen down his fiancé's throat as his ass strangled

Mark's embedded flesh.

The rush of passion would have been impossible to resist even if he'd wished to. Mark clung to his friend, his stare never leaving Sloan's gaze, and shot everything he'd held inside deep into Sebastian. He released of all the frustration, the inferiority, the jealousy.

He gave Bastian everything, and then some, coming until his cream squeezed around his softening cock, creating frothy foam between them. A dribble ran across his balls to the site where Lynn's lips connected to their flesh. She tasted them both simultaneously.

A final spasm wrung him dry. He blinked at Sloan, needing their connection.

The moment he could focus, their gazes met and held, Sloan cried out. Mark lunged forward, wrapping one hand around her upper arm, tugging her toward him until he captured her mouth in a violent kiss. He covered her breast with his other hand and manipulated her nipple.

Sebastian worked his magic tongue over her clit.

Together they extracted bliss from every pore of her body. Her eyes rolled in her head then she convulsed, spreading her saturation across Bastian's chin, cheeks and nose. He ate at her for long minutes until her cries subsided.

Then they all collapsed, like a pile of naughty puppies, on the bed. Together.

Sloan and Mark whispered the shared joy of their experience as they snuggled. Lynn and Sebastian relied more on touches to bring them down from the pinnacle of their releases. All four worked together to supply their lovers with what they needed most.

And right now, that was time to sort things out.

Sebastian and Lynn gathered their belongings then hugged Mark and Sloan. They whispered their thanks, promised to return when their friends were ready then headed toward their adjoining room, Lynn carried in the cradle of Sebastian's arms.

* * * * *

Sloan didn't know where to start. She'd been so terribly

misguided. What would her lover think when she told him how she felt now?

"Mark..." She cleared her throat and tried again but tears filled her eyes anyway. "I made a mistake."

The euphoria on his face died in an instant. "This isn't what you wanted after all?"

"No!" She jolted upright then surrounded him with her arms. "That's not what I meant. I was wrong to ask for time. I don't need one second longer to know this is what I crave. Forever. I didn't know what I really needed until I met you."

"Me either." Mark nodded. "I can't believe this is happening. All these years...but it wasn't until Bastian and I had Lynn and you that we were complete. If Bastian had never met her, if we'd never fooled around that night, if—"

"If I'd come along a few days later they would have approached you anyway." Sloan gulped, afraid of risking everything. But she couldn't assume he'd considered all the options. Finding out later that she wasn't necessary in the big picture would kill her. So she asked, even though the possibilities terrified her. "Would you like me to step aside? This evening...the magnetism we shared...it could be because of the relationship the three of you have. If you want to be with Lynn and Sebastian, I understand. You have a history with them. I want you to be happy."

Mark stared at her so long she couldn't believe he hadn't blinked, his expression completely unreadable.

"Marco?"

"Thinking."

"If it's that hard a decision, I should give you space to make the right choice."

"If you move one muscle I'll put you over my knee right now, Cougar or not." His intensity surprised and aroused her. "I'm considering my options on how to convince you I could never be happy without you. Fooling around with Sebastian and Lynn is scorching—and yes, more than sex because of our friendship—but I'm not a part of their relationship. And I don't think they're a part of ours. Not beyond friendship, respect and maybe some shared pleasure."

The weight of her anxiety grew lighter in her chest. Could

this be real?

"What I feel for you is…bigger than that. Sloan, I love you."

The rapid tattoo of her heart made it seem as though the organ tried to beat a response in Morse code. "It's crazy, I know. But I love you too."

Epilogue

Six months later

Sloan fussed with Lynn's vintage lace and pearl veil. They waited for the string quartet to begin playing the processional music from their spot at the top of the beach behind Sebastian's family home on the Amalfi Coast. Sloan couldn't image a more beautiful place to get married.

"Thank you for sharing this day with me." She stared at the bright blue sky to keep tears from ruining her makeup.

"If you say that one more time, I'm going to beat you with my bouquet." Lynn propped one hand on her hip, a knockout in her beaded, white-satin mermaid gown. "I couldn't imagine getting hitched without you and Mark here. You two are such an important part of our lives. Of us."

The bride gulped then sniffled.

"Oh damn, don't do that." Sloan hugged Lynn. "I'm sorry. I guess I can't believe how lucky I am to have friends like you and Bastian along with the man of my dreams. Sometimes it doesn't seem real, you know?"

"I have to say, I never expected to fly to Italy for a *double* wedding!" Rachel grinned as she came to the rescue with a box of tissues.

"Me either, but I have to say, I'm so happy for you both." Darci daubed some replacement eye shadow on Sloan then fixed the shell necklace draped over her bodice. "You deserve those two smoking-hot men waiting at the edge of the surf for you."

"Now quit this girly weeping shit." Larissa slapped Sloan on the ass. "We have two Cougars to give away. Your studs are waiting for a thumbs-up to start the ceremony."

"I still can't believe they all came." Sloan shook her head, wisps of hair dusting her face as she looked out over the crowd. Monica, Edie, Elle, Autumn, Stevie, Cam, Lori, Grace and the rest all looked unbelievably chic. Their young lovers gave the local Italian stallions a run for their money.

It had to be the sexiest collection of guests in attendance at a wedding ever.

Before the heaped blessings could inspire another ridiculous tear, strains of classical music drifted to Sloan's ears. A soft wind blew the sheer fabric draping the archway they'd placed on the beach and flower petals fluttered in the sand.

Lynn clasped Sloan's fingers in her trembling grip. Together they marched between the rows of white-painted chairs containing their friends and relatives. Love surrounded them but Sloan couldn't look anywhere but at Mark. He stood shoulder to shoulder with Sebastian.

The men grinned at each other then focused on the women they'd sworn their souls to. Two couples. Four friends. A mix of adventurous lovers bonded for life and beyond. Nothing could have felt more right.

Sloan couldn't wait to see what decadent surprises the two troublemakers had concocted for their honeymoons.

Thanks For Reading!

Did you enjoy this book? If so, please leave a review and tell your friends. Word of mouth and online reviews are immensely helpful to authors and greatly appreciated.

To keep up with all the latest news about Jayne's books, appearances, merchandise, release info, exclusive excerpts and more, sign up for her newsletter at

www.jaynerylon.com/newsletter

More than 25 prizes are given out to subscribers in each monthly edition.

SNEAK PEEK – *KING COBRA* – HOT RODS, BOOK 1

Want to read about more steamy car buffs? Have a thing for mechanics? If so, check out the Hot Rods series. But only if you have a thing for outrageously sexy ménages between open-minded garagemates with dark pasts.

An Excerpt from King Cobra

Chapter One

Eli London stared at the drop of sweat gathering on the shoulder of one of his mechanics, Alanso. He flexed his fingers around the torque wrench he'd retrieved for the man, refusing to let go and trace the path perspiration took over deceptively wiry muscles.

Inked artwork brightened as the bead dampened several tattoos. First a tribal scribble, then a portrait of Al's long-lost mom, and finally the top of an intricate cross that disappeared beneath the bunched fabric clinging around his waist. Torn and oil-stained coveralls hugged a high, tight ass.

All Eli could think of these days was that goddamned ass, which Alanso now shoved out in his direction while the bastard tuned some rich kid's engine. With hardly any effort at all, Eli could smack it. Or bite it. Or fuck it.

Son of a bitch.

Nothing good could come of this obsession. Damn his cousin Joe for putting crazy thoughts in his brain. The guy was a member of a construction crew that liked to work hard and play harder together. Their polyamorous bedroom gymnastics had become obvious when Eli and Alanso had walked in on a scene he couldn't forget. But just because that bastard had been lucky enough to find a whole team of fuck buddies his wife adored—

no, loved—didn't mean such a wild arrangement could work for everybody in the world.

Eli had no right to wish for the same. Yet lately, each time he looked at the half dozen guys and girl he considered his grease monkey family, he found himself sporting a hard-on stiff enough to jack up a tank with. Thankfully, the oblivious gang hadn't identified the source of his recent frustration. Though they certainly had borne the brunt of his bad temper, adding guilt to the unslakable arousal stripping his gears, leaving him spinning his wheels.

Stuck and stranded. Alone with his dirty little secret.

Except for Alanso

Why had that mechanic been the one to witness Joe and his crew's alternative loving along with Eli? Probably because they went most everywhere together. Eli shoved the memory of his right-hand man's right hand from his mind. Or at least he tried. The guy had tortured Eli's cock with greedy pumps of his trembling fist while the crew's foreman, Mike, demonstrated just how hot it could be to take on one of his own. By fucking Joe while the mechanics had stared, in awe of the power exchange.

Grunts had spilled from Joe's mouth, which knocked against his wife's breast as he took everything Mike gave him then begged for more. The audible decadence echoed through Eli's mind day in and day out. In perfect harmony with the memory of Alanso's answering cries as he witnessed the undeniable claiming.

Eli knew that if he slammed Alanso against the 426 inch engine block of that 1970 Dodge Challenger R/T coupe, the man would spread and welcome him.

Boss, friend…brother.

And that's where the fantasy turned to battery acid, burning Eli's insides with the bitter taste of responsibility and logic.

How could he want a guy he considered family? How could he violate that trust?

He couldn't afford to lose Alanso.

Not from his business, definitely not from his life.

So he could never seize what he craved. Frustration bubbled over.

"What's taking so long, Diaz?" Eli knocked thick, bunched biceps with the tool he carried.

"We're trying to make a profit here, you know?"

Alanso couldn't seem to wipe his glare away as easily as he rid his brow of the moisture dotting it. He snatched the wrench from Eli and returned to his task without taking the bait. If Eli couldn't fuck, the least the guy could do was give him the courtesy of engaging in a decent fight. His teeth ground together.

"You hear me, huevón? This isn't some charity case. Hot Rods is a business. Don't spend all day on a five-hundred-dollar job." Eli thumped the hood, knowing how the impact would reverberate.

Alanso's shoulders tensed. The clench of muscles along his spine altered the shape of his tattoos. Still, he said nothing about the low blow—or how he'd repaid the Londons a million times over for their hand-up through a solid decade of friendship and loyalty—and continued about his job. One he was damn fine at performing. No one could make an engine purr like Alanso.

"You want half-assed, go hire a motorman from the chain in town." He didn't bother to acknowledge Eli with a look.

Still, as Alanso's boss and best friend, Eli knew that tone well enough. It'd be accompanied by Al's tattooed middle finger sticking up along that wrench, he'd bet.

The defiance made Eli long to grab the other man's chin and force him to gaze up. Maybe then Alanso would see the desperation making Eli more unhinged than Mustang Sally during a particularly bad bout of PMS. God help them all.

He'd never wanted something he couldn't have so badly before. Except maybe to heal his mom during those horrid weeks she'd spent dying.

Terror and a soul-deep pain that never entirely faded turned him into something no better than a cornered animal. Eli lashed out. "Good idea. Maybe they'd spend less time checking me out and do their goddamned work."

A clang surprised him. He didn't quite realize what had happened until a spark flew from the metal tool where it connected with the concrete floor of the garage. Alanso had winged the thing an inch or less from Eli's thankfully steel-toed boot when he spun around.

He wouldn't have missed by accident.

"Para el carajo! Maybe I should've done more than look. You're obviously too hardheaded to man up and come for me. So the deal's off the table. I've wasted too much time on a dude who's in denial. You're right about that." Alanso sneered. "I'm tired of waiting for you to grow some cojones."

"Keep your voice down." Eli checked over his shoulder. Kaige and Carver didn't so much as glance in their direction, but the stillness of their bodies made it clear they caught at least wisps of the conversation. Years of tough living had taught the men to tread lightly in conflict. At least until swinging a punch became necessary. Then it was likely to become a free-for-all.

"Joder! Now you want to shut me up. Come mierda." Alanso scrubbed a hand over his bald head, leaving a streak of oil that tempted Eli to buff it away, maybe with his five o'clock shadow. "Wouldn't want the rest of the Hot Rods hearing about the good life and how we're not living it, right? They might revolt."

"Hey, I've never kept anyone against their will. You all chose to stay here. With me. The door's open." Eli waved toward the enormous rolling metal sheets that protected the garage bays at night or when the weather turned cold. Through them, the pumps of the service station his dad had started were visible.

A flash of something miserable twisted Alanso's usually smiling lips into a grimace. The gesture had Eli thinking of something other than what it would feel like to get a blowjob from the man. That was a first after weeks of studying that mouth.

He reached out, but it was too late. Alanso dodged, taking a step back and then another.

"You know what, Cobra." He grabbed his crotch hard enough to make Eli wince.

"You can suck it. Or, then again… No, you can't. That fucking checkered flag has dropped, amigo."

Reflex, instinct, dread—something—inspired Eli to lunge for the man who turned away.

Warm, moist skin met his palm.

"Get your fucking hands off me." When the engine guru pivoted, the unusual chill in his brown eyes froze Eli in his tracks. "You had your chance. You blew it. For us both. I'm out of here."

"You're quitting?" Eli gaped as the bottom fell out of his stomach. "Wait—"

"Hell no. I told you I'm over that bus-stop phase." Alanso sliced his hand through the air between them. His knuckles skimmed Eli's chest. They left a slash of fire across his heart. "I've got places to go and people to do. There are things I gotta learn about myself. And for the first time since we were fifteen, you're not going to be a part of that with me. Your loss."

"Shit. I-I'm sorry." Eli couldn't find a way to say what for. For violating their friendship, for wanting to destroy what they had or for acting like an ass by postponing the inevitable—he couldn't make up his mind. "Don't go."

They'd drawn a crowd. Even Roman inched closer now. The tough yet quiet guy stared openly at their spectacle. Charged air had somehow tipped off Sally too. She emerged from the painting booth, crossing the bays at an alarming rate. If she got tangled up in this, Eli would never forgive himself. Of all their gang, he knew better than to trample on her emotions. Her heart would rip in two if she had any idea of the rift opening at his feet right now.

Just like his chest was hewn.

"I'm not leaving leaving, Cobra." Alanso lowered his voice. "This is my home. I hope some things haven't changed. Let me know if I'm no longer welcome and I'll pack my shit. But I can't fucking do this anymore. Not for another damn minute. I have to know what it's like. To be honest about who I am and what I want. Before I lose any more respect for either of us."

"Fine then." Eli leaned forward before he could stop himself. The awful sensations sliding through his guts had to stop. Fast. Before the rest of the garage got caught in their crossfire. He shoved Alanso hard enough the man stumbled across the threshold before catching his balance. It felt like forcing a baby bird from the nest. He only hoped Al spread his wings fast enough. "Get the hell out. Do what you gotta do."

Alanso mouthed a plea out of sight of the guys now wiping hands on coveralls and milling near in a semi-circle. "Come with me."

Eli slammed his fist on the big red button on the doorframe beside him. With an ominous rattle, the metal door began to lower between them, severing all communication as completely as if the aluminum were a drawbridge over a monster-filled moat.

The scream of a crotch rocket taking off at an unwise speed ricocheted through their space. Gravel pinged when it slung against the barrier he'd erected.

"What the fuck did you do to him, Cobra?" Sally canted her head as she laid into Eli.

"You've really been acting like a snake lately, ever since Dave's accident. Hissing at anyone who comes near. We get that you're afraid of losing people important to you. The crew's near miss seems to have scared you stupid. I get it, I do."

He closed his eyes, trying to block out the concern she voiced for all the rest of the guys staring at him.

"But keep going like you are and you'll drive him away."

"Stop talking, Salome." He knew better than to tell her to shut up, even if she didn't understand how her insight cut him. Hopefully using her full name would be enough to convey how serious he was. He couldn't dive into the details.

No way could he admit what he and Alanso had seen. What they'd done.

"You better not have let your fear hurt him. Tell me you didn't." Her emerald eyes begged much more softly than her steely tone.

Eli didn't bother to lie.

The hand she let fly didn't catch him by surprise. She loved Alanso. They all did.
Which was why he didn't bother to duck. He deserved the stinging impact of her open palm on his cheek. That and more. Because even as his head whipped to the side, he admired the

stretch of her petite frame when she stood on her tiptoes, her raven hair and the glint of her fancy-painted fingernails, one of her pride and joys.

If he'd only wanted Alanso, maybe the two of them could have explored the possibility. But he was going to hell because he lusted after all of the Hot Rods.
The gang held their collective breath, waiting to see how he would react to Sally's uncharacteristic act of violence. Roman stiffened, prepared to spring to her defense.

All the fight leeched out of Eli.

No matter how bad it got, they didn't have to be afraid he'd attack one of their own. Then again, hadn't he done just that?

The damage he'd wrought would be far worse than the impact of a fist.

His shoulders dropped and his head hung. "I'll get him back."

"You'd fucking better." Mustang Sally shook her hand before propping it on her hip and pointing to the door. "Don't come home without him."

The five remaining guys closed rank around their littlest member. They knew she'd hate for Eli to see her tears or her alarm. He didn't waste any time offering comfort she wouldn't welcome. Kaige, Carver, Holden, Roman and Bryce would take good care of her.

They didn't need him.

But Alanso might.

ABOUT THE AUTHOR

Jayne Rylon is a New York Times and USA Today bestselling author. She received the 2011 Romantic Times Reviewers' Choice Award for Best Indie Erotic Romance. Her stories used to begin as daydreams in seemingly endless business meetings, but now she is a full time author, who employs the skills she learned from her straight-laced corporate existence in the business of writing. She lives in Ohio with two cats and her husband, the infamous Mr. Rylon. When she can escape her purple office, she loves to travel the world, avoid speeding tickets in her beloved Sky, and–of course–read.

Jayne loves to chat with fans.
You can find her at the following places when she's procrastinating:

Twitter: @JayneRylon
Facebook: http://www.facebook.com/jayne.rylon
Website: www.jaynerylon.com
Newsletter: www.jaynerylon.com/newsletter
Email: contact@jaynerylon.com

OTHER BOOKS BY JAYNE RYLON

Available Now

COMPASS BROTHERS
Northern Exposure
Southern Comfort
Eastern Ambitions
Western Ties

COMPASS GIRLS
Winter's Thaw
Hope Springs
Summer Fling

HOT RODS
King Cobra
Mustang Sally
Super Nova
Rebel On The Run

MEN IN BLUE
Night is Darkest
Razor's Edge
Mistress's Master
Spread Your Wings

PICK YOUR PLEASURES
Pick Your Pleasure
Pick Your Pleasure 2

PLAY DOCTOR
Dream Machine
Healing Touch

POWERTOOLS
Kate's Crew
Morgan's Surprise
Kayla's Gift
Devon's Pair
Nailed To The Wall
Hammer It Home

RACING FOR LOVE
Driven
Shifting Gears

RED LIGHT (STAR)
Through My Window
Star
Can't Buy Love
Free For All

SINGLE TITLES
Nice and Naughty
Picture Perfect
Phoenix Incantation
Where There's Smoke

AUDIOBOOKS
Nice and Naughty
Dream Machine
Night is Darkest
Report For Booty
Powertools
Kate's Crew
Morgan's Surprise
Kayla's Gift
Devon's Pair

Coming Soon

COMPASS GIRLS
Falling Softly

HOT RODS
Swinger Style
Barracuda's Heart
Touch of Amber
Long Time Coming

MEN IN BLUE
Spread Your Wings
Wounded Hearts
Bound For You

PICK YOUR PLEASURES
Pick Your Pleasure 3

PLAY DOCTOR
Developing Desire

SINGLE TITLE
Four-ever Theirs

Jayne Recommends…

Duty Bound

by Sidney Bristol
For more information visit www.sidneybristol.com

She's the woman he sent away.

Lisette wouldn't be back in New Orleans if she didn't need protection—and who better to turn to than her ex-boyfriend turned Detective? She's got a closet full of secrets that include a stalker ex and a kinky past. She vows to not dream about Mathieu…much. If only he were a Dominant, one who would not just flog her into bliss, but love her as well. A girl can dream, can't she?

He was her first love.

Mathieu wants nothing to do with another damsel in distress, but he can't say no when the little blonde woman walks back into his life with proof her ex is big trouble. He'll give her a place to sleep, but nothing more. His heart is locked up tight. Except, Lisette uncovers his past in the BDSM world and she's never backed down from a challenge. He can handle her, can't he?

Lisette and Mathieu embark on a relationship that is strictly about sexual gratification, but evolves into more. When the bodies align, the hearts entwine. Except their rekindled flame is in danger. Lisette's ex has found his prey, and he's not afraid of taking a life.

Contains a BONUS short story, Picture Her Completed.

Excerpt

Officer Mathieu Mouton sat at one of the four-top tables along the windows of Café Du Monde and gazed out at the darkening city, a sense of foreboding deep in his gut. The glitz and glitter of New Orleans stared back at him, like a young woman hungry for her beau. If it wasn't for his sister, Mathieu would have been at home flipping through the channels, scratching his dog, Gator's head, trying to put another week behind him.

Instead, he checked his phone again.

She needs your help, Mathieu.

He grimaced at the echo of his sister's words as she'd cornered him in their mamma's kitchen after the weekly family dinner. Damsels in distress were a dime a dozen in New Orleans and getting entangled in a charity project was not on his to do list. But no one said no to Lola. Not even grandmère. If Lola wasn't poised to take over the Assistant District Attorney spot opening up in the spring, grandmère would have made Lola a voodoo queen. It ran in their family since grandmère's grandmère.

The coffee in his cup was cold, the beignet untouched.

If this broad didn't show up in the next…

The café door opened and a bell chimed. A woman wearing a cherry red coat that covered her from knee to chin stepped in and shook the chill from her body. She carried a backpack that was stuffed until the seams strained.

Mathieu sat forward, propping his elbows on the table as he studied the patron.

She turned, honey blonde hair streaked with golden brown flipping over her shoulder as she surveyed the room. Her eyes snagged on him immediately and he sucked in a deep breath.

"C'est sa couillion." He was a raving lunatic.

No wonder Lola hadn't told him the name of the woman he was meeting. She started toward him. Even Mathieu could feel the cosmic pull between their two bodies. It's what had drawn him to her all those years ago—and was the reason he'd left.

"Mathieu..."

"Lisette Babineaux, haven't seen you in a minute," he drawled, rising to shake her hand.

Tricky, Lola. Real tricky.

Lisette's gaze flicked from his hand to his face before she put her small palm against his. Her skin was still soft and her nails were chipped, but painted with a pale pink polish. Despite the good quality of her clothing, it was dirty and worn. That didn't make sense. The Babineaux family was well off, and their little princess had never wanted for anything. But a lot changed in the years since he'd left her. He wasn't the same boy he'd been back then.

She'd always been delicate, refined, as if she'd stepped out of a painting of some debutant ball. Too fragile for a man with his dark tastes, but he'd hungered after her regardless. In his inexperience, he'd thought he could be a different man for her, one who didn't crave bondage with his women. He'd been wrong.

A handful of years hadn't changed her appearance all that much. Her hair was shorter, her eyes just as green, and the smattering of freckles preserved the air of youth about her, but there was a wariness to her that was new.

"I know. It's good to see you." She unbuttoned her coat and draped it over the back of her chair. Under the coat she wore a long-sleeved black shirt and jeans. Nothing too flashy, but it had never been her clothes that drew the attention.

"Have a seat, please." Mathieu didn't know what to make of the woman settling in across from him. They'd been something to each other once. "Lola tells me you're in a spot of trouble."

Lisette chuckled, a deep, husky sound that was music to his ears. "That's it? Tell me all your problems? No hello? Hi? How you been?"

Mathieu studied her, or more accurately, the woman she'd become. The black knit shirt, jeans and knee-high boots spoke of someone trying not to stick out, and yet she chose to wear a come-get-me red coat. Lisette was in trouble and didn't know how to handle it. If Mathieu listened to his cock, he'd take her home under the false premise of protecting her from whatever evil had her running. And then she would run from him.

This was a bad idea.

Another woman, not all that long ago, had needed his help. Her pleas for protection, promises of love and affection had dried up. She'd been out of his life barely a year, and he'd gotten drunk at the small apartment he and his dog now called home to celebrate; it had felt sad and pathetic instead.

"It's getting late. I'd rather we cut to the chase, if you don't mind." Mathieu would hear her out, give her some advice and send her on her way. The Babineaux family should be capable of taking care of their own.

Lisette blinked and her mouth worked soundlessly for a moment. She blew out a breath and shook her head, appearing to collect herself. "This is not how I pictured this happening."

"Right, sorry about that."

"Yeah, I'm sure you are." She pointed at his cup. "You drinking that?"

He shook his head.

"Do you mind?"

"Help yourself." He pushed the cup and pastry toward her.

Lisette gulped down at least half of the cold coffee before setting the mug down with a clink. She sighed and folded her hands on the table in front of her. He smothered memories wrapped in warmth of Lisette doing exactly this little act with her hands a number of times before saying something serious.

"You don't want to help me, do you?" Her gaze seemed to bore past his skin, straight to his soul, and for a moment, he was back on campus, sitting under the magnolia trees, a blossom in her hair.

Mathieu shook the memory from his mind. He hadn't seen that girl in a long time.

"It's not that I don't want to help you, but it seems awfully odd. Come to a cop, off duty? Wouldn't it be better if you went to the authorities?"

"You don't even know what's going on." She frowned.

"Exactly."

"Are you going to turn me down without even hearing me out?" Her voice rose as she spoke until she realized the few other patrons were staring and she ducked her head.

As a police officer, it was Mathieu's nature and conditioning to protect people, but he'd learned the hard way that damsels in distress were better served within the bounds of the law. He couldn't pretend he knew better. When it came down to it, he was part of a system of government that did its job when people allowed it.

"I'll give you what advice I can. I even know who's on duty tonight." Mathieu knew this decision was the right one; trying to save her would destroy him in the process. But he hated saying no to those cypress green eyes. It tore something out of him, and God knew he didn't have much left to lose.

Printed in Great Britain
by Amazon

25954873R00116